Praise for **Bracken MacLeod**

MOUNTAIN HOME

"Damn well worth your time. A tense thriller full of well-drawn characters and an imaginative setup that puts it all in motion. This guy's ready for the big leagues."
~ *New York Times Bestseller, Christopher Golden, author of TIN MEN and ARARAT*

"Next time some fool gleefully announces 'Small Press is dead,' tell him to read this stunning debut, a cut–to–the–bone novel that credibly interweaves the 180° range of the human spirit and the 180° of darkness below it. A magical book, a reflective mirror of truth ... and what that costs."
~ *Andrew Vachss, Raymond Chandler Award winning author of the Burke series*

"... with **MOUNTAIN HOME,** Bracken MacLeod has finally kicked the door right off the hinges. Thrilling, shocking, well-written, and with heart to spare."
~ *Kealan Patrick Burke, Stoker Award-winning author of THE TURTLE BOY, and KIN*

"... hits like a Claymore mine and cuts with the emotional precision of a scalpel. Ferocious and tender, painful and real, it shows that the worst horrors are those we create ourselves, and that this world offers no shelter from evil, not even for the innocent. A powerful and thoughtful first novel."
~ *Chet Williamson, International Horror Guild Award winning author of DEFENDERS OF THE FAITH and SOULSTORM*

"... brings heart and muscle to this taut siege thriller."
~ *Nicholas Kaufmann, Shirley Jackson Award-nominated author of CHASING THE DRAGON and DYING IS MY BUSINESS*

"**MOUNTAIN HOME** is a double barrel shotgun blast of violence and pathos. Clean, deft writing and more than enough narrative drive to keep you buzzing along, this debut marks the beginning of a very promising career for Bracken MacLeod."
~ *John Mantooth, author of SHOEBOX TRAIN WRECK and THE YEAR OF THE STORM*

"An unflinching look at the nature and implications of violence, **MOUNTAIN HOME** starts quite literally with a bang and keeps readers riveted until the last word."
~ *Nate Kenyon, Stoker Award-nominated author of BLOODSTONE and DAY ONE*

STRANDED

"A smart, surprisingly-moving, first-rate thriller that chucks Martin Cruz Smith's *Polar Star* down a *Twilight-Zone*-esque rabbit role."
~ Paul Tremblay, author of A HEAD FULL OF GHOSTS and DISAPPEARANCE AT DEVIL'S ROCK

"As brilliant as it is disturbing. Bracken MacLeod joins the ranks of today's top horror writers."
~ Jonathan Maberry, New York Times bestselling author of PATIENT ZERO

"Bracken MacLeod achieves the nearly impossible in **STRANDED**. He makes you feel claustrophobic in wide open spaces. The tension is the sort that makes breathing a challenge... One of the best suspense novels I've read in the last decade."
~ James A. Moore, author of THE SILENT ARMY and THE LAST SACRIFICE

"**STRANDED** is a genre-transcending triumph, proof that horror isn't about blobs-in-the-basement... it's about what's real (really) inside us all, and the pressure cooker of circumstances that brings that – all that – to the surface. With this book, Bracken MacLeod steps squarely into the highest rank of writers as he takes risks others couldn't hope to conceptualize ... and magically makes them work."
~ Andrew Vachss, award-winning author of The Burke series

"Stunning. MacLeod leads us on an existential journey through hell that moves smoothly from unease to horror, finding every emotional beat and giving full measure to each human hope and fear."
~ Dana Cameron, Agatha, Anthony, and Macavity award winning author of the Emma Fielding Archaeology Mysteries

13 VIEWS OF THE SUICIDE WOODS

"...although there's almost nothing of the supernatural in his superb new collection... MacLeod's fiction is full of traps – some physical, some psychological, none easy to wriggle free of."
~ Terrence Rafferty, THE NEW YORK TIMES BOOK REVIEW

COME TO DUST

"Bracken MacLeod's **COME TO DUST** packs punches on both a visceral and emotional level. Heart-wrenching and terrifying -- one of the absolute stand-outs in horror's new wave."
~ Brian Keene, bestselling author of THE RISING and PRESSURE

Also by Bracken MacLeod

NOVELS
Stranded
Come to Dust

NOVELLAS
White Knight

COLLECTIONS
13 Views of the Suicide Woods

for...

my grandfather, Claude, who taught me to love the stars,
and my son, Lucien, my morning star—the first light in my sky.

MOUNTAIN HOME

BRACKEN MACLEOD

Haverhill House Publishing

MOUNTAIN HOME © 2013/2017 **Bracken Macleod**
"Restored Edition" © 2017 **Bracken MacLeod**

Cover illustration © 2013 **www**.smalldogdesign.ca
Cover layout © 2017 **Dyer Wilk**

Originally published in 2013 by **Books of the Dead**

ISBN-13: 978-0-9779256-6-7
ISBN-10: 0977925668

First Haverhill House Publishing edition: October 2017

Published by

Haverhill House Publishing
643 E Broadway
Haverhill MA 01830-2420

Visit us on the web at **www.HaverhillHouse.com**

ACKNOWLEDGEMENTS:

Several people were instrumental in helping shape this book back when I first wrote it and to them I owe a huge debt of gratitude for their invaluable assistance and support. I must thank my Mad Dogs and first readers, Errick Nunnally and Christopher Irvin. They were the first ones to spend time in *Your Mountain Home Kitchen* and the book is stronger for it. Jan Kozlowski deserves special thanks, not only for being an early reader, but also for the effort she put into helping me refine the story and characters and for her commitment to making this novel the best it could be. All three of these people went above and beyond, and let me abuse a notion introduced to me by Ann Patchett at *the Muse and the Marketplace* conference in 2009: "No one you're not sleeping with should ever be asked to read your manuscript more than once."

To my influences, colleagues and, best of all, good friends, Christopher Golden, James A. Moore, KL Pereira, Paul Tremblay, Jonathan Maberry, Nicholas Kaufmann, John Mantooth, Chet Williamson, Brian Keene, Jack Haringa, Brett Savory, Sandra Kasturi, Michael Rowe, Adrian Van Young, Amanda Downum, Elizabeth Bear, John Dixon, Adam Cesare, Thomas Pluck, Gabino Iglesias, Kasey Lansdale, Joe Lansdale, Andrew Vachss, and Dallas Mayr, thank you for always being there for me.

No list of acknowledgements would be complete without singling out the late Papa Necon, Bob Booth. I owe thanks to Mama Necon, Mary Booth, as well and their kids, Sara and Dan. If it weren't for all of you and the entire Necon family I doubt I'd have written this, and I'm certain it wouldn't have ever been published. You all have my undying affection; you are my feast of friends.

Thank you, James Roy Daley, for your enthusiasm and for believing in the first edition of this book. Thank you, Joanne McKenna-Howard and Bill Howard at Small Dog Design for giving Mountain Home the cover I dreamed of!

My son, Lucien, is my sun and moon and stars. Without him, there is nothing bright in my sky.

Finally, my deepest thanks and unending love go to my wife, Heather MacLeod. Simply put, if it weren't for her, I couldn't write. She's my muse and my ideal reader. She's my inspiration for the women in this book who do what has to be done no matter how hard it is. And most of all, she's my best friend. "O wonderful, wonderful, most wonderful, wonderful, and yet again wonderful, and after that, out of all whooping!"

INTRODUCTION

by Chet Williamson

Back in April of 2013, I read a novella by a new writer I'd met the year before at NECON, the annual party convention for horror writers and readers both ancient and burgeoning. NECON is delightfully informal, with great opportunities to stand around, drinks in hand, and get to know folks.

One of those I got to know was Bracken MacLeod, a young man as hardy and hearty as his name, MacLeod of the Shaven Head, Inked Arms, Scribe's Beard, and "Jack Torrance Redrum" label t-shirt. In short, he blended in. But talking to MacLeod, I found him to be more than your usual horror geek. He'd been a trial attorney, taught college philosophy, and was a martial arts instructor, among other vocations, and that trifecta of law, philosophy, and ass-kicking made him one not to be trifled with, physically or verbally.

But the kid knew his stuff. We mostly talked books, and I found that this dude who looked like a biker extra from a Roger Corman movie was articulate, well-read, and precisely as intelligent as an attorney and philosophy professor should be. And he discussed writing in a way that made me think that he knew what was good and what was bad, though that didn't necessarily mean he could *write*.

We stayed in touch, and he later emailed me asking if I'd be willing to read a short novel (his first) for a possible blurb. I said sure, thinking that, if it was bad, I could always claim I just hadn't had time to get around to it (yes, all writers do that, and don't pretend you don't). Fortunately, I didn't have to resort to that shoddy strategy.

Mountain Home was terrific. I read it fast, because MacLeod made me want to know what the characters were going to do next, as opposed to what was going to *happen* to them next. There's a huge difference between those two literary strategies, and he knew it. The former is based on plot, and the latter is based on character, and it's those character-driven stories that truly resonate emotionally. *Mountain Home's* characters live. The main characters -- Lyn Lowry, Joanie Meyer, and Bryce Douglas -- are fully realized, but so is everyone else, even if they're "only" a victim. And some of the victims we haven't gotten to know receive their humanity posthumously through the grief of those who survive and mourn them.

That's the key to what makes this book as good as it is: MacLeod's acceptance of writer Philip Toynbee's realization that "other human beings are fully as human as oneself." It has nothing to with race or sex. Both the main protagonist and antagonist are women, while Luis (Latino), Neil and his son Hunter (African-American), and Leonard (Native American), are all individuals first and heroes or villains second. Not that there are true heroes or villains in this novel. MacLeod is never that simplistic. To say more would be to give the game away, and I don't want to do that.

There's a supernatural element here as well, but it's subtle, and seems almost metaphorical, as though it might help to explain the actions of the characters, even though there's no need to beyond their own humanity, and the strengths and weaknesses born of that humanity. Expect no *deus ex machina* or even a God of the Mountain to step in and change the game.

My final blurb was this: "Bracken MacLeod's *Mountain Home* hits like a Claymore mine and cuts with the emotional precision of a scalpel. Ferocious and tender, painful and real, it shows that the worst horrors are those we create ourselves, and that this world offers no shelter from evil, not even for the innocent. A powerful and thoughtful first novel."

I see no reason to change that opinion, particularly in the light of MacLeod's subsequent work: *White Knight*, a powerful *noir* novella; *13 Views of the Suicide Woods*, a short story collection that shows a wide variety of styles and subjects; and *Stranded*, an extraordinary novel of psychological terror set in the Arctic. And his newest novel, *Come to Dust*, sounds just as fascinating and involving as its predecessors, and I'm anxious to read it.

I've seen a lot of writers come and go, and I can count on one hand the number of new writers about whom I'm enthused enough to follow closely. And on my hand, Bracken MacLeod is that shaven, tattooed index finger that, when held up by itself, indicates that there can be only one. And his name is MacLeod.

I'm sorry. I was trying so hard not to go there.

Ignore my weakness if you can, and relish instead the strength of *Mountain Home*, one of the best first novels it's been my privilege to read, by a writer who should be around for a long time to come, if any justice remains in this mad and chaotic world.

Chet Williamson
July 17, 2017

MOUNTAIN HOME

BRACKEN MACLEOD

"People who don't have much get ugly about giving up the little they have left."

~ Andrew Vachss

PROLOGUE:

14 July 2013 — 1445 hrs

The asshole from table three paid with a credit card. Lyn Lowry read his name off of the front before handing it back along with the slip. "Here you go, Mr. Mills." Richard Mills smiled with half of his mouth and leaned over to sign the tab. While he figured out the tip, Lyn fingered the necklace dangling between her small breasts. She caught his eyes darting up to look at the sparkling silver faerie pendant she bought two years earlier at FantastiCon in Portland. After a moment too long, he straightened up and slid the ticket back to her. Lyn glanced down to see that in place of a tip, he'd drawn a horizontal line. She looked over his shoulder to where the new busboy, Luis, was clearing the mess they'd left. Grabbing her earring, she gave him the signal she'd taught him for "how much?" She hoped to see him hold up at least a five. Instead, he held up a single dollar bill and a bible tract and shrugged. *A buck on a thirty-dollar tab.* Lyn pushed the cash drawer closed gently, trying not to show her exasperation. Rick rhymes-with-dick Mills and his wife had not only been rude, but now they were also lousy tippers who thought she needed saving. *I've been judged by enough holy rollers at this friggin' job. Showing a little cleavage to get a better tip doesn't make me a whore. I'm trying to save enough for tuition, you losers!*

Instead of screaming at them, she kept her smile in place and said, "Thanks for eating at *Your Mountain Home Kitchen.*"

Mrs. Mills glanced over her shoulder with a haughty look that said she only spoke to the help when ordering something. She pushed the door open with her free arm, the other one squeezing the nasty yapping little dog they'd insisted on bringing into the restaurant—*you'll seat him too if you want our business, dear*—and stepped out into the afternoon sun.

Lyn imagined rich Rick and his wife getting into their Lexus convertible, taking the top down, and tearing down the road only to skid off the hairpin turn over near Mercy Lake and careen into the rocky valley below. She pictured the car exploding in a ball of flame like in the movies, and she smiled genuinely for the first time that day. Of course, she didn't really wish them harm. Maybe a little fishtail skid around the turn. Something to remind them that life was too short to be judgmental pricks.

"Y'all come back and see us agai—" A loud crack from outside the restaurant interrupted Lyn's farewell. She watched the golden halo of Mrs. Mills' bleach blond hair go dark and the back of her husband's head blow open like a crimson flower blooming in a time lapse educational film.

The mirror behind the cash register shattered and clattered to the floor in a rain of shards that bounced off the floor, pelting the backs of her calves. Lyn's world narrowed to the scene directly in front of her as Rick crumpled behind his wife, their bodies blocking open the glass doors leading out to the parking lot. Mrs. Mills' dog streaked away like a rat chased by a boa constrictor. Lyn tried to scream but the man's blood caught in her throat and she gagged. Her stomach rebelled at the taste. She stared blankly at the mess coating the register thinking, *Mr. McCann is going to kill me!*

The screams of the other customers sounded miles away.

Lyn wiped her mouth with the back of her blood-spattered forearm. She thought she might be screaming. But then, none of the customers in the café were coming over to make sure she was all right, so maybe she wasn't.

She looked up from the Mill's corpses in time to watch the plate glass window above tables five, six, and seven explode inward. Glass flew into the face of the man at table five who'd ordered a "bottomless" Coca-Cola. His head rocked violently to the side, but the prodigious gut he'd barely been able to squeeze into the booth held him in place. The bullet that blew most of his chins and jaw into the dining room ricocheted off to the right and grazed the woman from table nine before embedding itself in the cheap wood paneling below a framed picture of celebrity chef Paula Deen hugging the owner of the restaurant.

Lyn heard her own scream rising above the chaos like a siren. *Your Mountain Home Kitchen* was under attack.

PART ONE: JOANIE SETTLES HER TAB

1400 hrs

Joanie Myer stepped out onto her porch with her eyes closed. The warm afternoon air blew over the sheen of perspiration that coated her body. Carefully, she walked to the edge of the front deck, her hands grasping for the wooden rail she'd carved to replace the one that rotted out two summers earlier. The coolness of the breeze soon turned pleasantly warm as her sweat evaporated in the sun. She breathed in the scents of juniper and columbine, earth, lavender and lupine. Yet, over it all intruded the smell of the road: hot asphalt and exhaust. The spell was broken. There was no more reason to pretend. She opened her eyes.

She walked down the steps to her driveway. Her legs burned slightly and she reveled in the pleasant fatigue of a good workout—a ten klick run in the woods behind her house. Over the past three years she'd worn a circuit path through the woods that passed by everything she loved about her mountain home. *What do they call that path animals make?* She considered what her professor had said in the single class she enjoyed during her only year of college. *Paths of desire. They blaze paths of desire through their environment.*

Reaching the end of the driveway, she looked up at what had once been her favorite view in the world. The only vista she'd ever seen that rivaled it was the view of the mountains surrounding Bagram Air Force Base in Afghanistan. But *this* was home. *Had* been home. She stared at the giant neon sign topping the restaurant across the highway from her house. A range of Day-Glo mountains framing a little cartoon cottage in the middle shone like a beacon of tastelessness. Above that, tall western-style block letters proclaimed the diner to be:

<u>Your MOUNTAIN HOME Kitchen</u>

Below that blinked a smaller LED sign with scrolling crimson letters that read, *We're Open! Come On In!* Its obtrusive garishness infuriated her every time she looked at it. And she had looked at it every day since they'd erected the sign a year earlier. The restaurant itself had been bad enough, but her view of the lush pine valley below was now almost completely obscured by the continually lit sign. She could hear the hum of the neon buzz through her windows. That might have been the most maddening. It was inescapable, even when she pulled the blackout curtains. She'd never intended to hang blackout curtains. Not in *her* mountain home.

Resigned, she stuffed her clenched fists in her vest pockets and crossed the street. The highway had been a disappointment when she first moved into the house. But its minor inconveniences—the occasional sound of a truck or motorcycle making its way from Mercy Lake to Jasper's Fork along rural Route 1A—had been eclipsed by the house's seclusion and the dream view of the Selkirk Mountains outside her front door. Then dive-diner entrepreneur, Adam Bischoff, erected this cathedral of cheap chicken fried steak on a piece of property that would probably be lost to erosion in another ten years. She hadn't asked, but Joanie was sure he didn't care what happened to the restaurant that far down the road. He was more interested in driving her out of her home.

The parking lot was about half full. She counted nine cars. Three pickup trucks—two Fords and a Chevy—a Honda Civic, one of those new VW Beetles, two Subaru wagons, a BMW, and a 2012 Mercedes SLK convertible. A Subaru, one Ford, and the Civic belonged to employees. The Chevy belonged to the manager. The rest belonged to customers. The noisy gravel crunched under her boots as she walked up to the glass doors, pulled open the one on the right and walked in.

Inside, the hostess table was unattended. The nice girl, Lyn, was serving a couple in the back of the restaurant. She looked at the jingle of the bell and held up a finger in a *just-one-sec* gesture. When she saw it was Joanie, her finger and face fell. The man she was serving said something sharp and Lyn's head snapped back around to face him. The handbag dog his companion held gave a short yip and the couple sitting next to them—two women—tensed their shoulders. Everyone else was eating and chatting and minding their own business.

Lyn finished pouring coffee for the couple with the dog and hurried over to the lunch counter to set the coffeepot on the burner before greeting Joanie. The worried look didn't sit well on her delicate face. She had her hair pulled up from the sides and held back in a barrette that Joanie couldn't see but assumed was the same one she always wore. The ridiculous pink waitress uniform was designed for someone who could fill it out, not a lanky girl who built like a 1970s fashion model.

"Hey Joanie. Uh... Beau's here today. You know?" She never expected to be greeted with a *Welcome to Your Mountain Home Kitchen* like everyone else. Lyn only ever reported whether the manager was in the office in the back.

"S'okay. I just want a cup of coffee."

"If I get caught serving you again..." Lyn let her statement trail off.

"I can take it to go. I ran out at home."

Joanie waited while Lyn stood there trying to make up her mind, her face a mask of anxiety. After a few seconds, Lyn finally relaxed. "No. It's fine. There's a table in the back. I'll get you a cup and you can sit and enjoy it. *Screw them*, right?" She laughed humorlessly.

"Exactly." Joanie smiled, trying to help the girl relax. Adam was an asshole and he'd hired Beau to manage his restaurant because he was a real son of a bitch, too. Beau made sure everyone knew it, felt it, and feared him. At five eight in heels, he was a petty Napoleon in a bad western suit.

She followed Lyn into the restaurant. As they passed, a redheaded woman with a bobbed hairdo seated at a table in the middle of the dining room checked out her ass. She felt a flush of satisfaction as the woman's companion barked, "*I'm* over here, Carol."

The leathery old woman with the yappy dog sucked air through her teeth as she stared at Joanie's dirty brown desert boots. Her husband noisily slurped at his coffee trying not to burn his tongue. They sounded like a pair of Hannibal Lectors.

The table Lyn led her toward was the last one in the back, next to the hallway leading to the bathrooms and the side exit. Joanie guessed Lyn picked it in case she needed to make a quick getaway. No matter what, Joanie intended to walk out the front. "Be right back," the girl said.

"Take your time, Lyn."

The waitress slash hostess slash checkout girl ran off to fetch the same coffeepot she'd put down to greet Joanie. She grabbed a tan mug off the counter and hurried back to the table. She'd said, "screw them," but it was clear she knew who'd get screwed if she violated the *Do Not Serve Joanie Myer* rule.

"Black, right?" Lyn asked, setting down the cup and pouring.

Joanie smiled again. She liked Lyn. The girl reminded her of herself when she was twenty-one—full of energy and ambition and eagerness to please. But Lyn didn't seem to have any way to make her attributes come together. Joanie saw her either joining the military—like she had done when she flunked out of college—or, more likely, dying a waitress. "Thanks," she said, blowing on the steaming cup.

Lyn waited, squirming uncomfortably for a moment before saying, "Can I ask you something, Joanie?" She had her index finger nervously gripped in her right fist and looked about ready to twist it off.

"Sure. What?"

"What's with the combat boots? I mean, they're all hardcore and stuff but they don't go with the whole yoga thing, you know? I'm sorry. I know it's totally rude of me to say it like that. It's just, I want to go to school to be a fashion designer and I'm trying to learn why people make the kind of choices they make when they're getting dressed, and I—"

Joanie put her hand on Lyn's forearm to stop the flood. "It's okay. I'm not offended. It's weird, right?"

"Not weird. I don't know. Different?"

"I learned how to run in them in boot camp and haven't been able to get back into the hang of sneakers since," she explained. "You know what they say about old dogs."

"You're hardly an old dog." Lyn leaned in conspiratorially. "I think you might have just broken up those two over there." She nodded toward the women who were still having it out over tight pants and wandering eyes.

"Old enough to not want to give up what's mine." She leaned back. "Thanks for the coffee." She held up the cup and took a gulp of the steaming hot liquid, showing no sign that the drink was scalding hot as it rolled over her tongue and down her throat.

"You bet." Lyn smiled half-heartedly and rushed off to take the glass that the obese man in the booth by the front window kept banging on the table. "Another one?" she heard Lyn ask. The fat man replied, "Menu says it's bottomless. I can see the bottom, baby."

Joanie noted that he sat alone, wedged tight into the booth. She imagined that one of the beaten up pickup trucks in the parking lot was his. Probably the one with the silver girl silhouette mud flaps and the worn *You Can Keep The Change / Bachmann 2012* sticker on the bumper. Lyn brought him his soda pop and he downed half of it in a single greedy slurp. Joanie hoped she planned on getting him another right away.

Her eyes wandered over to the lesbian couple who appeared to have made up and were holding hands across the table. *That's nice,* she thought. She remembered Jules and Amanda serving with her in Iraq, during *Don't Ask Don't Tell.* Jules got discharged halfway through her second tour, even though she was one of the best Arabic speakers serving in the country. Amanda hid her true self much better and finished her stint with honor. She wondered if these two, sitting there holding hands, were thinking clearly about how they might be treated for PDAs in rural northern Idaho.

Lost in her thoughts, Joanie sat at the table with her mind trapped in a troop transport outside of Tikrit. Her face twitched at the memory. She didn't hear Beau hissing at her until the third time he said, "God damn it, Miss Myers. What are you doing here?"

"Oh, hi Beau."

"Don't 'hi Beau' me. You know you're banned from the premises," he said, unwrapping the cellophane from a fresh toothpick and sticking it between his teeth. She wondered why he'd decided to come out of his cave in the back when he did. Probably the busboy. Although she'd never said or done anything to him, he didn't appear to like Joanie. She'd caught him staring at her with a hostile look more than once. She imagined that it was part of new employee orientation for Adam or Beau (or both) to inform all male employees that she was not welcome under any circumstances.

"I'm just here for a cup of—"

"I don't care what you're here for, but I doubt it's for a cup of coffee. I swear, it's like you're trying to provoke our lawyers."

"I was thinking about staying for lunch. Do you know what's good on the menu here?"

"Christ on a cracker! Look Joan, I'd've been happy to buy you lunch for a month of Sundays if you'd taken the offer on the house. But since you didn't, Mr. Bischoff says you're banned from here." His jaw flexed as he chewed the pick.

Joanie drained the rest of her coffee and wiped her mouth before asking, "How much do I owe?"

"Free, if you get up and get out right now."

"I pay for the things I take."

"Oh, you'll pay. Just wait until the damage hearing on Mr. Bischoff's counter-suit. You'll buy us a damn extension on the place. Maybe we'll open a bed and breakfast on the other side of the highway." Joanie bit the inside of her cheek and concentrated on not punching Beauregard McCann. They'd have her house over her dead body. But then her lawyer had informed her that the judge had dismissed her harassment lawsuit and handed Bischoff his victory without either the expense or inconvenience of a trial. He'd scheduled the damages hearing for two weeks later—tomorrow. She hadn't figured her case to close the diner would get anywhere—hell, she'd *expected* it to be dismissed before a trial. The suit was about making Adam spend money, but the fact that he could buy a victory without her ever getting to say a word made her furious.

"How late are you working?" she managed to say without adding expletives or spitting in Beau's face.

"Are you asking me out on a date?"

"Just thinking about where I want to get dinner."

"Jasper's Fork is two hours up the road and Mercy Lake is forty-five minutes t'other way by the border. Take your pick."

Her seat made a loud scape across the tile floor as she stood to go, and several of the customers looked over at her She brushed past Beau roughly, knocking him a step back. *You might be alpha around here, but you don't scare me, little man. There's nothing you can do to me that's worse than what's already been done.* "You won't see me in here again," she promised.

"Don't let the door hit your ass on the way out, soldier."

"Airman," she said.

"Whatever. Just take those wings and fly."

Joanie made her way leisurely toward the door counting booths and the people in them. The woman with the dog snickered as she passed their table. The lesbians refused to make eye contact. And the fat man stared, licking his lips. A couple she hadn't noticed sitting at the first table inside the door motioned her over.

"We're sorry to stop you," the man said. "Did we hear that man mention you were in the service?" Unlike the others in the restaurant, she would have had a hard time putting him and his companion into an easy category. They dressed modestly and lacked eccentricities or even any memorable details. Man. Woman. Late thirties, maybe. Slim, healthy, good looking. She looked at their hands on the table. They wore matching plain gold wedding bands. No ice on her finger.

"Yes sir. United States Air Force. Twelve years."

"We wanted to say thank you for your service," the woman said. Joanie stood frozen in place for a moment. When she had first arrived at the airport in her BDUs she'd heard that often enough. People then were conscious of acknowledging that she'd paid a price for her country. Since dropping the uniform—and she *never* intended to put it on again—the gratitude had stopped.

"Thank you," she said. She reached for the wallet in the pocket of her vest. "Can I pay for your meal?"

The man's face clouded and he shook his head. "I think we ought to be buying you lunch."

"They won't serve me here," she said.

The couple looked genuinely offended—like they might get up and walk out, skipping on the check. "You're kidding? I guarantee we'll never eat here again if that's the case," the man said. He extended his hand. "My name's Jeff, and this is Sarah." Joanie shook his hand. His grip was firm, but he didn't squeeze too hard the way insecure men who learned she was former military often did. He let go and she shook Sarah's hand. Her grip was also warm and dry and strong. They both looked her in the eyes and half stood when they shook. Good people.

"I'm Joanie. Pleased to meet you." She pulled forty dollars out of her wallet and dropped it on the table. "I bet that'll cover it. Leave the rest as a tip. Lyn deserves better than what she gets."

"Honestly, we don't—"

"Please." She held up a hand. "Let me do this. Settle up and pay with this. Let's call it a little jab at them for not taking my money." Jeff and Sarah looked at each other and seemed to have a telepathic conversation. Together they said, "Thank you." Joanie could tell from the looks on their faces that they intended to pay their own bill and leave the forty for Lyn, who they had seen seat her and pour her a cup of coffee. That suited her just fine. She hoped Lyn would get the chance to spend it.

She took a step away and hesitated. "Excuse me. Which car is yours?"

"Why do you ask?"

"No reason. It's a game I play. I like to see if I can match people to their cars based on how they look. You look like Forester people. Colorado plates?"

"Yes. You're good."

"Lots of practice. Take care, people. If you're headed north, there's a hard curve up the road."

1419 hrs

Sitting on the stool behind the cash register, Lyn watched as Joanie chatted with the couple at table one. Beau was fond of saying to her, *if there's time to lean, there's time to clean,* but she half-expected Joanie to try to pay for the cup of coffee, so she lingered, waiting to check her out. She fought the temptation to pull her sketchbook out of the drawer below the cash register and work on a new drawing—maybe one of Joanie wearing a cocktail dress and heels instead of yoga pants and combat boots.

Joanie shook hands with the couple and exchanged a few more words that Lyn couldn't hear. She turned sharply on those clunky boots of hers and glided to the register. "You'd been here since open, right? Off soon?" she asked.

"'I'm stuck working till close. I was s'posed to be off an hour ago, but Deidre never showed up for her shift, so Beau's making me work a double." Lyn shrugged her shoulders. "It's more hours, right? More money for school." Joanie frowned. For some reason she couldn't discern, the news of Deirdre calling in sick seemed to upset Joanie more than she would've guessed.

Then, Joanie's expression seemed to shift from frustrated to sad. "More money for sure, but I'm sorry all the same."

"Sorry for what?"

Joanie stood for a moment looking her in the eye. It creeped Lyn out to be examined so intensely. But that was who Joanie was—intensity incarnate. Finally, she said, "Sorry you have to work so hard. Things ought to come easier to good people."

"It's okay. I don't mind hard work."

"I hope not. There's more of it for us than there is for them." She nodded toward the manager.

Beau stomped up to the register, clearly frustrated that Joanie was lingering when he'd tried to be as forceful as possible without making a scene in front of the guests. "I think I told you—"

Joanie glanced at the red-faced manager standing with his hands on his narrow hips and gave him a forced grin that stopped him in mid-sentence. She turned and walked out of the restaurant. "Take good care, Lyn."

Beau stood frozen with anger watching Joanie walk across the highway without looking left or right. Lyn held her breath. She could tell he was silently wishing for a pickup or a semi to come screaming along and run her over. When she made it across safely, he scowled. Joanie did something to Beau without even trying that no one else seemed capable of: she made him seem even smaller. Lyn smiled as she watched the woman ascend her driveway. Lyn resolved, later when she got around to drawing Joanie in the dress and heels, she was definitely going to try to imagine her smiling. This place didn't make anyone but Adam Bischoff happy. And Joanie deserved to be happy. She was a hero.

Beau hissed, "In my office. Now!"

"But the customers?"

"Let Luis handle them. He'll probably be replacing you anyway." Beau looked over at the busboy. In the two months he'd been working he hadn't done anything like an exceptional job. Beau crooked a finger at him and Luis sauntered over. "Kid. You've got the killing floor. Make sure everyone's drinks are full and if anyone orders anything, write it on this pad and take it to Leonard. We'll be back out in a minute."

Beau grabbed Lyn by the elbow and dragged her toward the office. As they passed the kitchen he barked at the cook to keep an eye on "the kid." Leonard nodded, looking a little worried that Lyn was being hauled into the principal's office.

At the end of the hallway, past the dishwashing station, the walk-in freezer, and the employee lockers, Beau opened the door to his office. Instead of shoving, he let go of Lyn's elbow and gestured like a fairy-tale prince asking her to the ball. She walked in and sat down, staring at her hands. She hoped that he'd fire her. Although waitressing wasn't rocket science, the work was exhausting. She'd never had a job that was so simple that she hated so much. If he let her go now, she could make the hour drive home and relax a little before she had to get started on dinner.

Beau took a seat behind his pressed-board desk and gave her a long look. The glass eyes of a stuffed deer's head hanging above him stared blindly at her. Below that, in a pine rack, hung the rifle that she imagined deadened the animal's gaze. Most guys kept their rifles at home or in a rack in their trucks, but Beau spent more time at the restaurant than his house. He'd appointed his small office like a personal den with trophies and other outward signs of his accomplishment men like him took pride in. Against another wall, a bookshelf sagged under the weight of lofty tomes like *The Psychological Foundations of Wealth* and *Making Business Work*. She never saw Beau crack a book, but it didn't surprise her that he had a collection of shitty self-help titles with unbroken spines. On his desk blotter sat a new one: *Miah "Matoskah" Walker's Taming the Shapeshifter: Aboriginal Strategies for Success*. The man pictured on the cover looked like twice the asshole Beau was.

Something he's aspiring to?

"What did I tell you about Miss Myers?" he asked.

"It's Myer."

"God damn it, Lyn! Now is not the time to be smart. What the hell did I tell you about serving Joanie Myers?" He shifted the ever-present toothpick from one corner of his mouth to the other, chewing on the wood. She thought about how much she'd like to snatch it and poke him in the eye with it. Banishing the thought, she acted properly cowed to please her manager.

"You said not to."

"That's right. Two god damn words. *Not to.* Are they so hard to remember?"

"No."

Beau folded his arms and leaned back in his chair. To Lyn it looked like he was trying to lie down. She wished for him to fall over backwards. She imagined if there was a part of his job he liked best (after kissing Adam Bischoff's rich ass) it was dressing down waitresses. "No, what?"

She knew he wanted to hear her call him 'sir.' "No, it isn't," she answered instead. "Are we done yet? Because Luis is probably scalding someone with coffee right now."

"No we're not done. You're on shaky ground, miss. This is going in your file. You want to use me as a reference ever in the future—and you might need references sooner than later if you keep this attitude up—you'd better toe the line. You know what that means?"

"It's from boxing."

"It means step up and do what you're supposed to." He leaned forward and put his elbows on the desk. "Get out there and do your job. And if the management decides to refuse service to anyone, then you god damn do what management says. Got it?"

"Yes." Beau didn't repeat his request for a 'sir.' Instead he dismissed her with a regal wave of his hand and an order to close his door on the way out. She hurried to the dining room, giving a clucking Leonard the finger and a wink as she passed the kitchen. He winked back, pointing his index finger and cocking his thumb.

Luis was indeed pouring coffee for a new couple seated along the far wall of the restaurant—a slender black man and a teenage boy who seemed to be in their own worlds. The fat man at table three was holding up his empty glass like it might suddenly start raining cola. Lyn walked up behind Luis, put her hand on his shoulder, and took the coffee pot from him when he was finished pouring. "Thanks," she said. "I got this."

"Yeah, sure." The way he hurried back to polishing the flatware, she knew that he'd probably been ready to jump out the window at the prospect of actual work.

Lyn began the process of catching up with the customer demands that accumulated every time she took a break. She often pictured herself in an imagined fantasy tavern—Brandybuck's. It sometimes made the hours at work move a little more quickly. She refreshed the steaming hot glögg for the couple from the Dark Lands and their yapping little pet goblin, refilled the dwarven miner's ale, and brought the lady wood elves their lunches. The human rangers at table one signed to her for the check. She dug it out of the pocket in the front of her apron and took it over.

"How was everything?" she asked.

"The food and the service were fine, but you can tell the manager that we won't ever be coming here again."

"I'm sorry. Is there something I can do to—" The man's wife put a hand on Lyn's forearm to stop her. Lyn hated being touched while she was working. Everyone always assumed it was okay to grab at the waitress when they wanted her attention and it made her skin crawl every single time.

"Don't tell your manager a thing, dear." She focused her attention on her husband. "You saw how he treated her just now. And you want her to go tell him that a couple of strangers from out of state won't be back tomorrow. *Shame* on you, Jeff."

"What? I don't like how they treated..." He trailed off after another unspoken communiqué from his wife. "Yes, of course you're right." He looked at Lyn who was debating whether she should walk away while they worked this out or stay and awkwardly wait for them to settle up. "The food was good and *your* service was great. That's it." He handed back the check with his credit card. Lyn took it to the register, rang it through, and returned with their receipt slip. "Thanks," Jeff said, putting his card away. "Can you settle a bet for us?"

"I don't know. I'll try."

"Are there bears up here?"

"Sure. A couple of years ago *Fish and Game* had to kill a grizzly that had gotten used to eating people-food out of dumpsters. It's why we have to keep ours padlocked."

"Grizzly!" Sarah said.

"Yeah, but that's the *only* one I've heard of around here. Mostly it's black bears. Why?"

"Sarah says she saw a bear—"

"A *giant* bear. Like a grizzly."

"A pretty big one on our way here. But I think it was too big to be a bear.

I was thinking it was maybe an elk."

Lyn laughed. "Well, both are possible, I guess—this place is out in the middle of nowhere—but it's kind of hard to confuse a bear and an elk. One's, like, got antlers."

"I *saw* antlers."

"I saw a bear standing underneath tree branches and so did you," Sarah said playfully. "Elk don't stand on their hind legs."

"Where did you see... whatever it was?"

"A half mile that way." Sarah pointed out the window in the direction of Mercy Lake. "It was standing on the side of the road."

"Yeesh! I like them both better on TV," Lyn said. "Too big and scary in real life, you know?"

"We hear you there," Jeff said. He and Sarah smiled, seemingly satisfied that they had seen something in the woods, whatever it was.

"Sorry I couldn't help you settle the bet." Lyn headed for hostess station and missed seeing Jeff slipping Joanie's pair of twenties with the check slip under the salt and pepper shakers. The couple got up, collected their things and walked out the door. She looked up and, as instructed, said, "Thanks for eating at *Your Mountain Home Kitchen*." She was supposed to always add, "Y'all come back and see us again," even though she'd never sincerely said "y'all" once in her life. No one in the area talked like that, but Beau thought it sounded "folksy." She thought it was hokey. Either way, they'd already said this was their last visit. Though she hoped it wasn't. They were nice people. She saw too few of those lately.

1425 hrs

Luis sauntered over to bus the newly vacated table. Looking over his shoulder at Lyn, he watched her busying herself, straightening the hostess station. As she bent down to stuff the spare menus below, he spied the pair of twenties under the salt and pepper. He looked at the slip and saw they'd added twenty percent as well. It confused him to see both a tip on the tab and forty dollars, cash. He pocketed the money and put the check back. Lyn stood up and smiled as she caught him looking over his shoulder at her again. He returned the smile and wondered if what Beau said about her was true. She had a figure like a boy, but he'd still love to see those lips wrapped around his cock.

1426 hrs

Leonard Blackbear tapped Lyn on the shoulder and she turned around startled, her focus shifting to him from whatever distant land she had been surveying through the glass doors. He stood towering over her. "If everyone's all set," he said, "I'm headed out to have a cigarette." In reality, he had a customer coming to buy a little weed and was going out back to wait for them.

"Yeah. Everyone's good, except for the guy with the ten-gallon bladder over there." Lyn nodded toward Bottomless Coke. "I'll come get you if anyone wants anything from the grill." He knew she saw through his lie. She didn't mind. She was sweet and he gave her a friends and family discount when she needed a spliff.

"Thanks." Though he liked her better than anyone else at Your Mountain Home Kitchen, that was close to the longest conversation they'd ever had. Separated as they were between the kitchen and the "killing floor," as Beau called it, if she wasn't calling out an order, they communicated mostly in teasing hand signals and winks. "Oh hey," he said. "You dropped this when the bossman dragged you to his office." He held out the hardcover Moleskine sketchbook she kept in her apron pocket. She took it from him, clutching it to her chest with crossed arms like a shield. "Can I see?" he asked.

"Huh?" She appeared to be trying to shake off a momentary disorientation.

"Your sketchbook. Can I take a look? I've seen you drawing in it when business gets slow, but you've never shown me anything you've done."

"I don't usually... show people my stuff. It's not that good." She tried to hug the book a little tighter.

Leonard kept his hand out, not demanding, but hoping that she'd open up a little and share. He could see she was struggling today, and thought if she didn't catch a break she might crack open completely. Every time she opened the sketchbook, it seemed to take her someplace better. He wanted to go there too, if only for a moment.

She handed the tablet over and looked at her feet like she was waiting for the inevitable advice to not quit her day job. He flipped open the first page to a sketch of a lithe young woman wearing an ensemble not unlike what Lyn was usually wearing before changing into her uniform—like something an elfin warrior would wear to go night clubbing in New York City. "Nice work," he said. She didn't reply. The next couple of pages were more of the same straightforward sartorial illustrations with more attention paid to fashion than artistic experimentation. Then he came to the portrait. Lyn had drawn a three-quarter profile of him.

Though he came and went from the Kitchen dressed for work with his hair in a net, she'd drawn him with his braids down, like he was on break. She'd been kind in her representation, yet she'd still captured the little wrinkles around his eyes and mouth he noticed in the mirror, that she couldn't have possibly seen all the way from the front of the restaurant. Her attention to detail impressed him. She had to have been studying him in the small moments when she'd hang an order on the spinner or pick up a plate. He held up the picture so she could compare it to his face. "No one has ever drawn me before. How do I look?"

"Sorry," she said without looking up.

"Don't be. I think it's excellent."

Her face brightened a little. "You really think so?"

He regarded her with a look that said he didn't pay empty compliments. She smiled. Leonard flipped to the next page to find a portrait of someone who must have been a customer at one point. It was a man sitting, staring out one of the windows at the house across the street. Again, her attention to detail was startling. He held the page closer and thought he might have been able to see the silhouette of the woman who lived on the other side of the highway.

The next two pages were more flat, urban fantasy clothing designs. He turned the page and nearly fumbled the book. Staring at him was a chimerical beast—mostly bear, but with a leering wolf's head topped with a stag's antlers. The monster's slavering mouth hung open revealing teeth that—even in pencil—seemed to glisten on the page. Leonard held his breath.

She looked up at him and a worried expression passed over her face.

"What? Which one?"

He struggled to find the word.

"*What?*"

"This one looks like a scary story my grandfather used to tell me about. *Kreewatan* is what he called him. He has other names from other people, but that's the one I remember my granddad using."

She pulled the sketchbook out of his hands and closed it. With a trembling voice, she said, "I made this guy up. I had a dream about him."

His smile shrank. "Dream or no dream, that's *Kreewatan*." Leonard felt conflicted. He liked Lyn and wanted to explain, but the picture frightened him badly. *So much for distractions.* "He's a fringe figure that appears after westward expansion. Like the ghost dance people thought would bring the buffalo back and rid the land of the Whites. The *Kreewatan Cult* started with the *Paiute*, but spread as a new religious movement through native communities around 1880. He was worshiped from the *Abenaki* in Maine to the *Yakama Nation*. They believed that the only way to be rid of the white man was to invite *Kreewatan* to their lands."

"So he's a protector?" she asked.

"Not at all. He's a spirit of destruction. Kind of like an animistic atom bomb."

"So he comes and takes out everyone you hate?"

"When he comes, everyone goes mad and kills each other. He's a harbinger, kind of. But he's also an agitator. *Kreewatan*'s coming means that the whole world is about to end. At least, the whole world for the people who see him."

"How do you know all this? Because you're Indian... Native American?"

Leonard looked at the kid with a touch of exasperation. "I know this because I have a Master's degree from University of Washington in American folklore."

"No shit?"

"No shit."

She blushed hard and slumped her shoulders as if saying something so stupid was physically shrinking her.

"Hey, it's okay. My grandfather told me that back when he was in grammar school, he appeared to him in a dream right before a man set fire to their dormitory. Thirty-eight boys taken from tribes all over died because some *wašicun* with a gas can and a Zippo hated American Indians. My grandfather was a *Codetalker*. When they liberated Dachau, some of the prisoners told him they saw him. They called him something else—something in Hebrew, but it was the same spirit."

Lyn shook her head. "I don't believe in that sort of stuff. Gods and spirits."

"Do you believe in lightning? In the stories, *Kreewatan* is a force of nature like that, or fire. Not a god. You can harness it, but if it gets away from you it'll consume everything. And sometimes it just happens, even when you don't do anything."

"How do you get rid of him?" The expression on her face was remorseful, building toward panicked.

"You don't. You can put out individual fires, but that doesn't get rid of fire, does it? You survive if you can. You work together and survive." He gave her a reassuring smile. "Hey, it's okay. A drawing is just a drawing, right? No need to get weirded out. It's not like you dreamed about him. Go out and do your thing. The day'll come to an end and you can go home and enjoy this." He pulled a hand-rolled cigarette out of his pocket and handed it to her.

She held up her hands. "I don't have any extra cash this week. My mom's been out of work."

"Consider it a thank you for letting me look in your book. I think you're really talented. You should keep drawing." He held the joint closer. "See if this inspires you."

Lyn took the joint and slipped it into her apron pocket. "Thanks." The big man turned to head outside for his smoke break. "Hey, Leonard," she called out after him. Did you ever see a bear up here?"

The big man stopped and turned around slowly. His smile faded and he simply looked sad. "A couple of times. They're not around like they used to be. Why?"

"The couple who just left said they saw a grizzly." She hesitated. "Or maybe... an elk."

He huffed out a breath of air that sounded half like a laugh and half like a moose snort. "They couldn't tell the difference?"

"They thought they saw different parts."

He was reminded of the parable of the blind men trying to describe an elephant. He tried not to think of her sketch.

"Were they locals?"

"No. From out of state."

"They probably saw a tree stump." He winked at Lyn as if to say, city folks wouldn't know the difference and walked away to have his smoke.

1426 hrs

Joanie sat at the breakfast table in front of the picture window that looked out on *Your Mountain Home Kitchen* and filled in the diagram she'd started the night before. *The Coloradoans are seated at the first booth by the door––they'll be leaving soon—the redhead and the jealous woman are at the table in the middle of the restaurant, 'Fat Fuck' is in the fifth booth from the door by the picture window, and the couple with the dog is at the table near him. Finally, the last customers to go in were the quiet man and his teenage boy in the booth along the wall. Employees: The busboy likes to hang back and polish tableware by the soda-machine and the cook is in the kitchen where he belongs. Lyn moves around the floor, but when she stops it is usually at the register near the door. And Beau. Beau is locked in his office like the fucking coward he is.*

Is that everyone? No one at the counters. It's late for lunch and early for dinner. It was probably busier this morning, but that run felt so good. She thought fondly of her extra long morning run to burn off the nervous energy of her pre-dawn excursion down the mountain. She'd been determined to let the calmness of the woods settle deep into her body and mind before going into the diner to do reconnaissance. She'd been very disappointed to discover that Beau had held Lyn's shift over again. *She was supposed to be gone as soon as the lunch rush was over. Then that other girl comes in. The one with the whorey makeup and the boyfriend who keeps a twelve pack of Bud Light under the front seat of his Mustang.* Another regret. But at least the couple at the first table wouldn't add to them. As soon as they got in their car and left, she'd head to the "hide." From there she'd try to figure out a way to let Lyn go if she could.

A glint of sun from the glass door opening and closing across the highway caught her attention. She heard the faint jingle of the bell above the doors each time anyone entered or exited. Until now, it had never sounded like a starting bell. *Ding ding. Ding ding. Fight!* She watched the Coloradoans walk with their arms around each other to the green Subaru crossover SUV. He kissed his wife before she got in and then continued around to the driver's side. They acted like newlyweds but their telepathic link was too strong for anyone only married a year or two, she thought. *Lucky them.*

She wondered if it might be a good idea to call Bryce one last time. Put things off until tomorrow. Hear his voice. Invite him over. Feel his breath. *No. It's too late for that. The hearing is tomorrow. It has to be now.*

Joanie reached down to run her fingers through Hoshi's soft white fur. The kishu-inu lay at her feet tail wagging. He looked at her with the eyes that she loved second only to Bryce Douglas' and panted. Through the open window she heard the sound of the Subaru driving off in the direction of Jasper's Fork. "That's it. Time to get started."

Taking the forty-five from the table, she put two rounds in the dog. "I'm sorry, Hoshi." One more regret to add to the day; she was going to need both hands to count them all before she was done.

1442 hrs

Looking in her sketchbook at the fantasy creature she'd dreamt about, a feeling of unease crept into Lyn's guts. She stared at the wolf-bear-elk chimera that had haunted her the night before, and Leonard's words about his grandfather's dreams echoed in her brain. *Just a dream,* she reminded herself. *It's not real.*

The woman with the dog sucked air through her teeth impatiently to signal Lyn for the check. She slipped her sketchbook into the drawer underneath the cash register and headed over to their table with the check and a warm smile. "Is there anything else I can get for you folks?"

"The bill we asked for five minutes ago." The mutt yipped at Lyn as if to punctuate the woman's sharpness. They hadn't asked for the check, but Lyn apologized anyway.

"Here you go, guys. My name's Lynnea and it's been a real pleasure serving you today."

"Service? Is that what you call it? Whatever the owner is paying to keep his bad reviews off of Yelp is worth every cent."

"Sir? I don't think I understand."

"I'm saying that when we checked out this place online it didn't quite prepare us for the kind of experience we actually had."

Lyn tried to parse the man's passive aggressiveness, but was too tired to want to go diving deeply into his mind. "I'm so sorry if your meal or the... service wasn't to your liking. There's a space on the back of the check where you can leave your comments and contact information if you'd like the manager to get in touch with you."

She tore the ticket out of her pad and held it out. The man stared at her, silently dismissing her. Lyn took the hint. She set the bill face down on the table and returned to the cash register. She cast her eyes around the restaurant looking for signs that other customers needed her attention before she got locked to the station cashing these jerks out. Everyone seemed to be settled in well enough—even Mr. Bottomless Coke. She took the moment to try to relax a little. The day was becoming a nightmare and she still had six hours in her shift. At least when this rush cleared out she could ask Leonard to fix her something to eat. *Worst job ever. Just six more hours, Lyn, and then you can get some sleep and use the day off tomorrow to start looking for another job.* If there was any luck in the world, it was that Adam Bischoff only owned one restaurant in Mercy Lake. She wasn't interested in anything else he had his fingers in.

Out of the corner of her eye she saw the couple with the dog get up, collect their bags, and walk her way. *All right, Lyn... time to turn on the charm! Earn your money.* She tried to put the frustrations of Joanie and Beau's pissing match out of her mind so she could improve her tip. She checked to make sure that her blouse was undone enough to show the hint of cleavage she didn't really possess, but not to look like she didn't know how to dress herself. It was a fine balancing act. *One last chance to earn your keep, and then they're gone forever, sweetie.*

PART TWO: JOANIE GOES TO WAR

14 July 2013 — 0259 hrs

In the moonless dark, she looked up at the night sky. The stars were thick as sand on a beach. Faint colors peppered the white pinpoints of distant, ancient suns, and a nebulous Milky Way arm arced overhead to disappear into the tops of silhouetted trees towering around her like a wall made of void. She stood gazing up at the history of the universe, light from stars first burning billions of years ago bathed her in luminescence birthed in violence. This was why she lived on the mountain.

In town in the valley below, as small as it was, the glow from street lamps and porch lights, traffic signals and billboard spotlights dimmed the stars, hiding more than half of them in the incandescent haze. Light pollution, they called it. It blocked out the stars. When she'd stayed with Errol in Boston, the nighttime sky was an almost featureless stretch of blue. She could only see Venus and Mars and the moon, not this rich, black curtain of diamonds. She tried to imagine herself floating among them. Staring at the northern Idaho sky above her was as close as she'd ever come to space travel as a terrestrial being.

She breathed in. The crisp night air cooled her lungs and she tasted columbine and earth. The smells of countless pine needles coating the forest floor competed with the odor of trees whose bark, scored open by deer antlers and bear claws, bled sap. No diesel exhaust or hot asphalt overshadowed the fragrance of the natural world, though the stench of incendiary chemicals and burning oil were never far from her memory. The tranquility of the night stood in contrast to everything that raged in her mind. The light rustle of a breeze in full branches above. A quick scrabbling in the brush below as some nocturnal creature scurried away into darker spaces—

running away from the scent of her on the breeze. In her memories, the echo of mortar rounds and small arms, the drone and storm of Humvees, planes, tanks, and IEDs. The sharp crack of her rifle, as steady in her ears as the sound of a metronome.

As she stood in the civilized clearing of the back yard with the house looming behind her, she thought, *I can just walk into the woods and disappear. I don't have to be here. I don't have to do any of this.* The wildness of the quiet nighttime world beckoned. But this was the line she'd drawn for herself—standing at the start of things that couldn't be undone. In that moment, she existed in the liminal space between possible worlds. A retreat toward the woods was the genesis of one reality, while a step toward the house made her the mother of an entirely other future. And in between, she waited. She waited for her heart to tell her to leave the house behind, and accept the world as it came to her. But her heart didn't beat like that. Her heart beat in the world of spilled blood and roiling smoke. Fire and death. The one where getting her way meant pulling triggers. A step into the quiet wild was never a possible future for her; she was foolish to imagine it.

She turned toward the house and crossed the lawn. At the top of the steps to the back porch, she reached for the doorknob. *No one out here locks their doors,* she thought as her hand closed around it. That was supposed to be a good thing.

Instead, it was the beginning of the end of everything.

She turned the knob and she stepped through the doorway into the house. Inside, it was silent in a way entirely unlike the broken, restless quiet of the outdoors. The new stillness spoke of tight confinement instead of the freedom of a grand expanse. Her breathing caught as her memories shifted again to the heat of a steel box baking in the desert sun. The smell of rust, bleach, and body drifted across her recollection. She felt the muscles in her abdomen and thighs tighten as she clenched her teeth and balled up her hands into fists. *Just a memory. Everything is just a memory.*

She crept toward the staircase and up the stairs to the master bedroom. Beyond the door at the end of the hall, he saw him asleep in bed. He snorted and stirred. Her heart skipped a beat and she stopped, waiting for him to sit up and look at her. Instead, he turned his head the other direction, snorted again and exhaled, long and slow. She stalked across the carpeted floor, pulling the syringe from her pocket and uncapping the needle. She knew the prick of the jab would wake him, but the sedative would put him back down just as fast. She hoped.

She opened the drawer and took a look at the gun he'd try to use to kill her if it didn't. *Justifiably so.* No lock. Loaded with a round in the chamber. She stuffed it in her jacket pocket and leaned over to give him the injection. The woman next to him lay on her side, facing away, breathing slow and deeply. Joanie would deal with her after. She hoped there wasn't another gun in the other nightstand.

1315 hrs

Deputy sheriff Bryce Douglas pulled his cruiser into the parking lot of the *Idaho Loggers' Association Credit Union*. He sat in the car for a moment before radioing in his position and turning off the ignition. Carlotta squawked through the radio, "Checking in on the little lady?"

"Yep," he replied. "Back in two minutes."

"Treat her right, Bryce. Take five."

"Ten-four. Bryce out." By one o'clock he figured she should be back from lunch and at her desk. He wasn't sure of her schedule since the promotion to loan officer—an advancement she'd received *after* kicking him out of the house. He unscrewed the cap off the plastic water bottle in his cup holder and spat a brown line of viscous tobacco saliva into it. He recapped it and put it back. So far, in a regular patrol, he had yet to completely fill one.

He walked into the pleasantly air conditioned lobby and, by force of habit, headed toward her old spot along the customer transaction wall. He stopped when he didn't see her standing at her old booth and scanned the room for a desk with her name on it. He'd never really noticed before that all of the desks were behind short privacy walls. He couldn't find Cherie's new station.

"Bryce, how are ya?" He jumped a little as the bank manager spoke from over his shoulder. He faced the man he'd arrested twice for DUI. In a town like Mercy Lake where the guys at the paper mill worked hard and played harder, you had to be more than a little bit of a menace to get busted for driving drunk. There were too many of them and only him, Chet Carey and

Jorge Rivera—the other deputies—to keep the peace when the sheriff went to bed early on weekends. The last time he saw Jacob Nance, the man had totaled his *Expedition* over by the courthouse and was wandering the street pulling on door handles trying to find another car he could "borrow" to get home.

"Just fine, Mr. Nance. And you?" Jacob fished around in his front pocket and pulled out a green token. Holding it up, Bryce saw it was a three-month AA sobriety chip. *There's no such thing as anonymity in a small town.* He wondered which of the drunks he hadn't run in for a while was Jacob's sponsor. "Well, I'll be damned, Jacob. Lookin' good."

"Feelin' good. With the help of the Lord and my family I aim to earn a whole collection of these." Jacob returned the chip to his pocket and stood for a moment looking like he expected Bryce to take the news of his prolonged sobriety and walk right back out the door. "You lookin' for Cherie?" he finally asked.

"Yessir."

"She's in the third carrel. Don't keep her long. We need her in the game. She knows how to close a deal like nobody's business."

"Thank you kindly." He walked a little shakily to the low walls surrounding his wife's desk, uncertain whether he should knock or try to playfully peek over the top. He elected to knock. "Cherie. You in there?" He could see through the frosted window that she was.

"Bryce?" She stood up to peek out at him. "Come on in." He stepped through the gap in the carrel and sat in a low, uncomfortable chair that reminded him of a doctor's waiting room. Cherie sat back down in her fancy ergonomic swivel chair.

"How've you been?" she asked.

"Fine. And you?"

"Just fine, as you can see. So far I've made loans to..." She smiled. "Well, it's not for me to say—confidentiality in lending and all. Two truck purchases and a house re-fi. It's been a pretty good first week."

"I'm glad to hear it." They sat in uncomfortable silence. It reminded Bryce of the long formerly comfortable silences they used to share sitting on the sofa watching television after the kids had gone to bed. Him enjoying another beer, and Cherie sipping a glass of white wine. They'd done that for close to ten years. And then one day she found a motel receipt. That's all it was. Not a chat transcript, not a boudoir photo or a pair of souvenir panties. Just a receipt for a siesta check in to the Sleepy Inn out on Route 4. Cherie knew he had no need for a motel. The county wasn't that big and his duties kept him in town for the most part.

Dishonesty was a hard burden for Bryce to bear. He'd been sleeping with another woman, but he carried the guilt of it from the first moment he flirted with her and let the weight pile up on him every time they slept together after that. As the weeks became months, he became a little more stoop-shouldered under the burden. He was certain that he'd unconsciously kept that receipt in his trouser pocket for exactly the purpose of getting caught. It was an escape plan—one poorly conceived, but then, Bryce Douglas was better at reacting than planning—a perfect patrol cop. Always a deputy, never a sheriff.

"What else do you want to hear?" she asked.

He'd come to the credit union looking for an order from a superior. "When I can come home. I miss the kids."

"You see them every day after school." Cherie wasn't exactly cold. He could see that she loved him, but her disappointment was plain. Comfortable silences had been dealt a deadly blow.

"You know what I mean. I miss our home. I miss us."

"Did you miss us when you were betraying your wedding vows up at Sleepy's?" Bryce had no answer. He had no explanation other than that his loins had gone wandering and his head followed like a teenager who only conceived the consequences of his actions as they were starting to take shape.

"I'm sorry, Cher. How long do I have to pay for one bad bet?"

"Oh, it was a *gamble* was it? I thought you said it was a mistake?" Her eyes narrowed as she studied him. Looking for a hint that his remorse was dishonest.

"That's not what I meant."

"Well in these terms, you have to play this hand until you're square with the house. How does that sound? Now I have to get back to work. Your next ante up is to figure out what you're going to fix the kids for supper. I'm not getting out of here until late."

"Does that mean I can come home?"

Her eyes narrowed in a warning. "For dinners. Let's start there and see if you can handle the responsibility."

"Thank you."

"Don't thank me." Cherie paused while she studied her husband. He felt her gaze penetrating him, looking for faithlessness. "Thank the kids. *They* convinced me to try this. I wanted to call Steve Pullman." He almost choked at the mention of the lawyer.

Bryce liked Steve. He'd reluctantly arrested him a couple of years earlier for beating the holy hell out of a guy who had casually backhanded his girlfriend in a bar. They'd gone out for breakfast after Steve made bail. He got the charges dismissed and afterward they'd become casual pals—not the kind who fish together, but if they ran into one another it could turn into an hour of coffee and catching up. Bryce knew his friendship was ephemeral, however. Steve had told him that he went into law to punish men who treated their women badly—the way his daddy had done to his mother. Once Steve knew about Bryce's infidelity he would no longer consider him a friend; Bryce would be another notch in his gun.

"One more thing," Cherie said.

"Anything," he promised.

"Have you faced up to what you did to *her*?" He, of course, had not. As soon as Cherie confronted him about the receipt, he dropped his lover without a word, ignoring her calls on the CB. He'd even stopped going up Route 1A on his patrols. The diner would have to look after itself. Shame wouldn't let him go up that road.

"I think you need to be very clear with whoever it was..." Cherie had told him that she did not want to know the identity of his mistress. She couldn't face the idea of running into her at the grocery store or the salon and having to pretend to be nice. It didn't matter to her if everyone in town knew but her. And she was adamant that she was not going to help Bryce carry his guilt around. Better not to know. "Very clear, that you have done both me and her wrong, that you are sorry, and that you are finished. For good. You got it?"

Bryce nodded. As usual, Cherie was right. He'd not just hurt one woman. He thought of the ten-year chip in his dresser drawer. Once a year he drove over to Portland to attend a meeting—to mark the years since he'd gotten his life in order. But now he was back on his steps.

He needed to make amends.

He needed to head up the mountain to Joanie's place.

1443 hrs.

Joanie lay down on the blanket spread over the cool hardwood platform she'd built. It had taken her longer than she'd anticipated getting it perfectly sturdy, but she had accomplished the goal in time. She picked up the Remington M24 rifle and carefully extended the bipod legs. Resting her cheek lightly against the butt stock, she flipped up the lens caps on the scope. Looking through it and the diaphanous black drape she hung in front of the window facing the restaurant—completing what snipers called "a hide"—she trained the crosshairs on the glass doors to the diner. The air outside was still. Without any wind to correct for, she calculated drop at a hundred meters and settled in for the wait.

She had hoped that the lateness of the day would mean a minimum of customers in the restaurant, but *Your Mountain Home Kitchen* was becoming ever more popular as word spread among people who both worked and played along the points connected by the scenic highway. It was about as deserted as the place was going to get until they closed late tonight. But if she waited until they closed, then Adam Bischoff wouldn't have a chance to understand exactly what the consequences of his actions were. He needed to be shown that it doesn't matter who you think you are. Everybody pays.

Through her scope she saw the woman with the handbag dog walk to the cash register. Her husband's back was turned and provided a perfect target. Except the doors were closed. The glass might distort her first shot, and Lyn was directly in front of the man. Joanie's 7.62mm black tip ammunition was designed to pierce twenty millimeters of hardened steel at one hundred meters. She knew that the ammo was overkill, but anticipated having to shoot through obstacles like overturned tables and perhaps the lunch counter. Plus, the windows were meant to withstand the kind of weather that pummeled the mountain in winter. Her shot was definitely going *through* that man into whatever was on the other side of him. He bent down, she assumed, to sign the check. Through the scope, she saw Lyn looking at him, forcing a smile, while he decided whether or not he'd pay her fairly for her service.

What are you doing, Joanie? Are you insane? Because this is fucking crazy. She had been trained to find her target, aim, and shoot with mechanical indifference. In three tours as a counter-sniper she'd put down six men; all righteous kills—justified takedowns of bad men trying to do harm to good people. She'd done her duty and protected the assets under fire.

This was murder.

Just pack it in. Eject the round and pack up the rifle. Then go into the living room and take your dog out back and bury him. Give up on giving up. There's nothing else to do now.

She watched the man signing the check look at Lyn's chest. Lyn looked a question over his shoulder, tugging her earlobe. Her face fell; the smile replaced by a look of disappointment that meant the house lights had gone up and the show was over. Joanie felt herself soften at the sight of the girl looking at once both so sad and unsurprised.

I give up. She slid her hand from the grip, intending to do the sane thing and rack the bolt lever to eject the chambered round. And then it happened. The woman with the dog turned around with a smile on her face, her husband following behind, laughing. The two of them filled with joy as they exited the restaurant into the light. The cross dangling from the woman's wrinkled, sun-damaged neck glinted in the daylight.

2009 — Time Unknown

He thrust into her again, grunting as she shrieked, the cross dangling from his neck glinting in the light of the LED lantern he'd set up inside the shipping can. He pumped in and out and that cross swung back and forth and she screamed and screamed. For mercy, for help, for him to let her go. And all he did was fuck and laugh, scrunching his face as he moaned, "Oh yeah," and "Oh god." He came inside the rubber and gave her one last thrust shoving his bony hips between her bruised thighs. His necklace batted humiliatingly against her forehead.

"You know, you're getting better," he said as he pushed off of her. "I figured you'd get with the program after a while. Fuckin' frigid dyke."

She pulled up her knees and tried to curl into a ball. Her muscles cramped and she arched her back, kicking out with one leg, grazing the mercenary's knee with her bare foot. "You fuckin' bitch!" The zip ties held her arms together at the top of the cot while he punched her in the gut and then in the face. She caught a glint of gold below one knuckle that exploded in a flash of white as she mercifully lost consciousness.

14 July 2013 — 1445 hrs

The woman with the dog stepped out the door of *Your Mountain Home Kitchen* into the gravel parking lot. Joanie felt herself break as she pulled the trigger. She imagined sailing forward, riding the bullet like a missile hurtling into oblivion, slamming into that stupid fucking face and pushing through her brains and out the back of head, through her teased up fake blond hair. She flew with the round into the man behind her—his head exploding in a red cloud of stupidity and bad intentions. Joanie returned to her own body to see the lifeless couple fall to the ground through her riflescope. She felt like someone ripped out of a shining white tunnel by doctors who'd returned her from the brink of death—cheated out of paradise. She tracked to the right to find the fat man trapped in the booth like a god damned beached whale and pulled the trigger again. This time she stayed put and watched her round do its job all on its own.

A bullet has no conscience to consult as it flies from the barrel of a gun. It doesn't feel the wind or the sun or the rain as it speeds toward its target. It penetrates the innocent and the guilty with equal intent and creates victims with the same enthusiasm with which it saves them from the bullets of others. No feelings of regret or elation occur to it as it tears skin, breaks bone, rips through organs, and frees blood to flow over them all. A bullet is the ultimate punctuation: more final than a period, more forceful than an exclamation, and never a question. A bullet is only potential and, after fired, it settles into eternity as a dead heap with no future. And the gunman's hand, having writ in fire and smoke and blood, moves on to send another round to follow along.

In the distance, Joanie heard a deep, throaty howl echo through the mountains. The sound chilled her blood as she settled in for the work ahead.

1445 hrs

Lyn choked and sputtered on Richard Mills' blood and nearly fell down in the spatter of glistening gore, bone, and grey matter in front of her. She screamed in concert with the sound of crashing glass, though it took her a moment to realize the sound was her. Another watermelon whump of exploding bone and brains followed a half second later by the thin thunder peal of a rifle crack. Growing up in Idaho you couldn't mistake the sound of a rifle, although this was no twenty-two or thirty aught six. The women sitting together at table four shrieked and ran for the bathroom hallway. Another shot smashed through a window and one of them fell, her face skidding along the tile floor. Lyn's panicked mind repeated, *What is happening? Jesus Christ, what is going on?* but all she could do was scream.

"It's coming from the parking lot!" the man sitting with his son at table seven shouted as he grabbed the boy and dragged him under the table.

"What the fuck?" Luis called out.

"Behind the counter! Get behind the lunch counter!" It was Lyn shrieking that last. Others might have thought she was instructing everyone to take cover, but she was really trying to convince herself to move. She yelled again as she staggered out from behind the register looking for somewhere safe to hide. "Get down, everybody get the hell down!" She slid into the space between the counter and the kitchen and huddled up, trying to make herself as small as possible.

"Syl! Sylvia! Oh god, oh fucking god help me get her in here!" The redhead from table four was trying to drag her girlfriend behind the counter, but the limp woman's hip was caught on the edge of the coffee machine and she couldn't pull the body around. More shots. More breaking glass. Lyn crawled forward and was nearly crushed under the collapsing racks of coffee mugs and dessert plates that toppled over as Luis hurdled the counter, bouncing off the far wall. She reached the redhead, grabbed her under her armpits, and pulled as hard as she could. The limp woman's body wrenched free of the teetering coffee station and together they hauled her back. A hole the size of a soft ball had been torn out of the woman's right breast. Her mouth was filled with blood and she clearly wasn't breathing. "Help her! Somebody help her!" the redhead screamed.

"I don't know what to do," Lyn sobbed.

"Call 911. Somebody call somebody!" The redhead cried.

"Mine's broken," Luis shouted. He held up the pieces of the phone that had shattered as he crashed into the wall behind the counter. "Anyone else got one?"

"My purse!" The redhead pointed to the dining room.

"Mine's in my locker in the back, but I never get a signal up here," Lyn said.

"Where's the landline?" the woman demanded.

"By the register," Lyn answered, pointing. That phone hadn't rung all day. She usually answered two or three calls a shift from townies or tourists wondering if they were open for supper. Today, nothing. "But it's right in front of the door where..." She wanted to say, "Where those shitty tippers got shot," but she couldn't bring herself to vocalize it. She remembered her wish that they lose it around the hairpin curve up the road. *I take it back! I don't want anyone to get hurt. Please! Stop this!*

"Syl," the redhead sobbed. "Please don't leave me. Someone has to call the police."

Lyn crept to the far edge of the counter and peeked around. She expected to see the gunman standing in the doorway of the restaurant, rifle in hand waiting to pick her off. Instead, all she saw were bodies. *I can't do it. I can't do it.* There was a break in the line of windows between table one and the cash register where a brick wall, featuring a local artist's painting of wild horses hung above the gumball and salted peanut vending machines. To discourage dine-and-dashers, the register was in sight of the doors, resting on a narrow counter that stored menus, phonebooks for both Mercy Lake and Jasper's Fork, and the night deposit bags. The phone hung on a hollow plywood wall behind the register. It would be impossible to get to the phone without being seen. Opposite the dubious cover of the plywood wall, were swinging doors leading to the kitchen and Beau's office all the way in the rear. There were no windows on that side of the building and a single steel door, which led out to the back lot—the only place anyone could usually get a cell signal.

A sign hung in the front of the diner advertising the lack of mobile service as a feature of the restaurant. *Come dine in an environment where your social network is at the table instead of in your hand!*

Her heart pounded in her chest so hard she thought she might die without ever being shot. Frozen, she struggled to catch her breath. *You can do it you can do it just fucking do it people are dying.* As she worked up the will to leap toward the swinging doors, Beau came bursting through them. "What in jumped up hell is going on out here?"

"Get down!" Luis called out.

"Lynnea, what the hell—" The rifle report cut off his question and Beau hit the floor. Lyn screamed again. "Jesus H. Christ!" he shouted as he crawled behind the counter with the others.

"We've got to get to the phone," Lyn said.

"It's dead," Beau declared. "Has been all day. I've been on my cell trying to get the company out to look at it, but my signal shits the bed every time I get them on the line."

"What do we do?"

"I don't know," Beau said.

"Syl is dying." The redhead held the dead woman's head; a mouthful of blood trickled down her chin. "We've got to help her." No one replied. The truth seemed too difficult to put into words. "Please. Will someone please do something? I don't know what I'll do without her." She slumped over the body and wept.

Lyn curled behind the counter, pulling her knees to her chest. "She's right. Somebody has to do something."

"What do you suggest, Lyn? There's only one way out of here and that's the road between us and..." Beau trailed off as he realized what was happening. His eyes went big and round as the last trace of bravado drained out of him.

"What? What is it, *jéfé*?" Luis said.

"It's Joanie Myer."

Luis was blinking his eyes so quickly Lyn thought he was having a seizure. Instead, he said, "Who the fuck cares about Joanie Myer? Someone out there is trying to kill us."

"*She's* the one shooting at us, moron! She's a god damned Air Force sniper."

"Dude, fuck that. I am getting out of here." Luis got up on his haunches like he was ready to spring over the counter the way he'd come.

"How? Which way?" Beau shouted.

"The back, man. She can't see out that way. I'll go down the hill and then climb back up to the road when I'm far enough away."

"You ever look down the mountain behind this place?" Beau asked. "There's no way out."

"It's forty-five miles to Mercy Lake, Luis," Lyn added. "Even if you make it through the forest to the road, it'll be hours before you get back. Let's wait her out."

"Bitch, my cousin's a sniper in the Marines. He told me that one time he waited three days to get the perfect shot on some sand nigger. No sleeping, no eating, pissing in his pants. *Three* days. We can't wait her out."

"Luis is right. We can't wait."

"But what do we do?" Lyn asked.

Beau blinked. His head trembled as if he wanted to shake it but couldn't work up the will to move more than a tremor. He raised a trembling hand and pointed over the counter. "For starters, one of us is going to have to drop the blinds over those windows so she can't see in," Beau said.

"I ain't doin' it," Luis said.

"We'll draw straws," Beau said. "Short straw pulls the blinds.

"Fuck that, man. Straw or not, I said, I ain't doin' it!"

Luis settled down, giving up on his idea of scrambling down a sheer rock cliff into the untamed mountain forest below. When he had first been hired, Lyn thought he was cute. As time went on, his true nature shone through in bits and pieces. A short tip here, a hateful joke there. He wasn't about to put his life on the line for her. Who would? Of all the people working there, Leonard was the only one who was more than indifferent toward her. But she couldn't hear him over the argument between Beau and Luis. He wasn't behind the lunch counter with them. She imagined that meant he was either dead in the kitchen or hiding like they were. Aside from him, no one in the restaurant was anyone she could count on to cover a shift, let alone to risk getting shot to keep her safe.

She looked over at the cash register where she'd been standing when the first shot came. *I stood there like a startled deer, staring out the front door. She wouldn't even have had to re-aim the gun to kill me. Instead she moved on to the guy with the Cokes.* The truth dawned on her then: *Joanie likes me. Out of all of these people, the only one who I can count on is the one shooting at us.*

"I'll do it," she volunteered.

"Yeah, fuck it. Let her do it."

"No," Beau insisted. "It's a bad idea. We should all go into the back and wait for the cops."

Lyn got up on her haunches. "I was standing out there in the open in front of that wall the whole time she was shooting and she didn't kill me. I'll do it."

Beau looked confused, but she could see in Luis' eyes that he followed what she was saying. He'd watched Joanie stop and talk to her. He'd seen her serve coffee to the killer. He knew that she was right.

"Let her do it," he said.

1500 hrs

Bryce had felt a pull like hers once when he got bounced into a river during a whitewater rafting trip. He was lucky enough to miss the rocks when he went in, but the current dragged him into an eddy pool and down he went. The rushing water turned him over and upside down and around so he couldn't tell which way back to the surface. He struggled to break free, but the power of it held him in place, choking the life out of him until a hand reached in and pulled him up and out.

Joanie felt like that.

When he saw her in her yoga pants and her tight shirts, hair pulled up in a practical but girlish ponytail, he felt like he couldn't get any air. She just had a hold of him.

You can have Joanie and alimony, child support and visitation, or you can have Cherie and your old life. It should've been a no-brainer. Cherie was the love of his life. They'd met in high school and he'd pursued her for two years. It took a lot of doing, but eventually he won her over with charm and determination. These days, he'd have been called in to the principal's office (or maybe the police station) for stalking, but back then it was how you wooed a girl if you were a little too skinny guy who didn't like to play football. He gave her flowers and candy, cute stuffed animals and notes—so many notes—just to prove that he wasn't another one of those guys who wanted to bed her and move back to the cheerleading pool for another flavor. He wore her down and finally she relented and agreed to the date he'd asked for so many times. And then he got another. And then they were "going out." He gave her a "promise ring"—a childish pledge to be engaged to be engaged. Then they got engaged for real as he entered the Peace Officer Standards and Training program and she went to U of I in Moscow for college. They married at twenty when she quit school and moved home. She gave him a daughter when they were twenty-one, a son at twenty-three. And that's when they grew up. Now, he needed a new set of adult tools to make his marriage work. No more promises of promises to come.

By contrast, he needed nothing to be with Joanie other than a stiff cock and the energy to keep up. The latter was harder than the former. Joanie had get-up-and-go for days. She could out run, out gun, and out fuck him. And when she did any of those things he felt like he was eighteen again. But, of course, he wasn't eighteen. He was thirty-five and had two kids and a lovely wife and a good job and he had put it all in jeopardy, for what?

Gifts and sweet notes weren't going to work if he wanted to hold on to the one person who'd stood by him when he was undergoing chemo for the cancer in his testicle at twenty-seven—the same year he was sued by the guy whose arm he broke making an over-enthusiastic arrest in a bar fight. Cherie had stood by him again a year later, after he'd beat cancer and had almost died in the river instead. He'd had to go the hospital again, even though the co-pays on the chemo had eaten up all of their savings. Cherie had been the one holding him up when he wanted to lie down. And now he needed to stand up on his own and take responsibility for what he'd done.

He radioed in that he was going off the clock. His shift was over and it was time to head to Joanie's to say his piece and maybe even pay a little for the wrong he'd done.

1500 hrs

Lyn peeked around the corner of the bar. The task seemed impossible. The ties holding up the blinds were all the way across the restaurant, through a sea of broken glass and directly in the line of fire. She wasn't convinced Joanie would spare her indefinitely—just that she hadn't killed her *yet*. It was a bet everyone was willing to take, but she wasn't a gambler. Even the thought of playing nickel slots made her nauseous.

"Go on," Luis egged.

"Give me a minute."

"Why? So your girlfriend can pick the rest of us off?"

"That's enough, Luis," Beau said. "You're going to do your part whether you like it or not. Once Lyn gets those blinds down, you're going out the back to see if you can get a signal with whatever phones we can find out on…" Beau's face screwed into a grimace, and it appeared to Lyn that he suddenly thought better of referring to the dining area as the "Killing Floor" like he always did. "Whatever phones we can find out there," he finished.

"Whatever, man," The busboy said.

Lyn leaned out a little further from cover. She didn't hear anything, but she didn't die either. "I'm going." No one said anything. She would have liked to have heard "good luck," or "be careful." Any expression of encouragement would have done. She looked back one last time, hoping that Beau would tell her to stop, saying he'd go in her place. Instead, he gave her a thumbs-up.

The redhead sat weeping and mumbling sweet nothings to a dead woman.

Luis just stared at her.

Clutching a dishrag she kept under the counter for wiping up spills, she crept out into the dining room and headed for the short wall by the doors. Once there, she turned toward the first set of windows. Across the dining room, she saw the man and his son huddled together beneath the booth at the far end of the restaurant. She felt relieved to see more people alive. It gave her a little hope. The boy was hiding behind his dad who was holding up his hands for her to stop. She ignored him.

I can't stop now.

She brushed some of the glass that had sprayed out from the exploding windows away with the rag. A jagged shard poked through the thin cloth into the side of her hand. "Shit!" She recoiled and pressed her lips to the puncture. "Be careful, stupid," she mumbled through a mouthful of hand and silently wished for one of the heavy-duty cooking mitts from the kitchen. The thought made her recollect one of her grandfather's favorite sayings. *Lyn, you can wish in one hand and shit in the other and see which one fills up first. Or you can use those hands to make something happen. Choice is yours,* he'd say.

I can sit back and wish for the police to show up and save us all, or… Or what? Or I can crawl through twenty feet of glass and try not to get shot saving a couple of jerks who hate me and a bunch of complete strangers. The boy peeked around his father's shoulder at her. They exchanged a few words she couldn't hear.

"What are you doing?" Beau called out.

"There's all sorts of glass out here. I don't think I can do it."

"You have to. Oh god, you have to," the redhead cried out. Lyn closed her eyes and sat for a minute working up the nerve. *It's up to you, Lynnea. Like always. Like when Dad ran off with the slut and you put off school to work full time so the rest of you wouldn't get kicked out of the house. Even though that asshole Brian was old enough to get a job and help out, too. Then, he went off to college and left you behind with Mom, waiting tables. Waiting. For what? For Mom to climb out of a bottle and say, 'I'm sorry, hon. It wasn't fair to ask you to do* everything.' *What am I waiting for? If I sit still long enough I'll die never having done anything I wanted to do, just like Grandpa. Vietnam and then two jobs forever and selfish kids and then prostate cancer a year before retirement. Two years of chemo and getting his balls cut off and then screaming at the hallucinations from his bed because no one would prescribe him enough drugs to keep the pain away. All for what?* She looked over her shoulder. Beau and Luis were motioning for her to go. *So I can save* them? *Screw that. I'm going to do it so I can get out of here alive. I'm doing this for myself. Right? I'm going to do this.*

When she opened her eyes again, she wrapped her hand in the dishrag and slowly pushed against the glass lying on top of the carpet. The big shards moved aside, but several smaller pieces caught and stuck in the fibers. It occurred to her that she didn't have to go on hands and knees yet. She crouched up, knees together—her skirt too tight to allow her to really duck-walk—and inched forward on the balls of her feet. Lyn felt exposed enough without hiking the skirt up over her hips so she could have a full range of movement. Glass crunched as she went; she could feel it stabbing into the bottoms of her sneakers. She held her breath and hoped the soles were thick enough nothing would stab through.

She was too tall to stay on her feet and not have her head poke up above the tops of the tables. She'd have to get on her hands and knees eventually. Lyn thought about her jeans wadded up in the locker in the back of the building. She hated driving to work in her uniform. For a moment, she contemplated heading back to get them. *They probably won't keep me from getting cut up, but they'd be a hell of a lot better protection than panty hose.* She looked at the swinging doors. Although the plywood wall blocked the view straight through, from where Lyn squatted they were in plain sight. *How did Beau get out here without getting shot? If she wants to kill anyone, it has to be him. What's she waiting for? What if she's gone around back?*

She pictured Joanie stalking them around the restaurant, either waiting for them to come out the rear or coming in to get them herself. The back door was only locked after hours—Beau didn't trust anyone but himself and Leonard with keys. *She could walk around behind the place, let herself in, and murder us all.* Lyn sat and listened, wondering if she'd be able to hear Joanie creeping around the building through the gravel.

"What's going on out there?" Beau called out.

"Shut up! I'm thinking."

"Thinking about what? Get the god damned blinds down."

Lyn looked at her first target. The ties for the windows over the first two sets of booths were only a few feet away in between stations two and three. But she had to crawl up into a booth to untie them. Those were the easy ones. Twenty feet farther along, at the end of table five, hung the next set of blinds. And she'd have to crawl over a corpulent dead body to get to them. With him in the way, it looked impossible. At least Bottomless Coke had finally stopped asking for refills.

She glanced at the man and his son underneath the table. Although the space was small, and there was barely space for an adult and a spidery teenage boy who was all arms and legs, they were out of sight of the windows and had plenty of solid wall between them and Joanie's bullets. The father stared at Lyn shaking his head.

If Joanie's in the front, this is the only choice we have. If she's in back, this is worthless, but what else can we do? Abandoning her dream of getting her jeans, she returned to brushing away as much glass as she could before crawling out, careful to keep her head below the booth tables. Although she was clearing the large pieces of glass, the embedded smaller shards were biting and slicing her knees and shins. Lyn's palms burned with pain from where the glass slivers dug into them. She stopped to look at one of her hands. The blood wiped away by her movement across the carpet came pilling up in dozens of tiny little dots of crimson, staining her whole palm red. She wanted to stop and suck on her aching hand, but knew that she'd get glass in her mouth if she did. She moved forward another two feet before having to stop again because of the pain.

"You have to know this is a bad idea," the man beneath the table called out. "I know what you're trying to do and you should go back."

"I have to get the blinds down."

"He's going to kill you before you can untie them."

"No she won't. It's a she."

"Okay. *She.* Just stop right there. Please! Before you hurt yourself any worse."

"I have to do this," she said, tears blurring her vision. She didn't know how much more pain she could handle. "She's not going to shoot me." Lyn didn't believe the words even as she spoke them. She didn't know why she ever had believed in Joanie's mercy. Joanie hadn't killed her *yet*, but that didn't prove a thing.

"Shut the fuck up, man!" Luis called over the counter. "Let her pull down the shades!"

"I have an idea," the man said.

"No, dad! Don't go out there." The boy held tighter to his father. The man gently pried his son's fingers away from his arm. The kid couldn't have been more than thirteen or fourteen, but he looked wiry and strong. Lyn figured if he wanted to hold his father back, the older man would have a tough time getting away.

"It's okay, Hunter," he said. "She needs the help and I have an idea." He looked at Lyn. "Do you want to stand there untwisting the lines, or would you rather cut them?"

She didn't want to do either. She wanted to be home in bed listening to *Russian Circles* or *Mono* on her headphones and working in her sketchbook. *It's going to be a while before you draw again,* she thought, looking at her hands. She carefully pulled a sliver of glass out of the heel of her palm and tossed it away. The dull pain was becoming a hot ache that was creeping into her wrists.

"Cut them?" she asked. "With what?" The man pulled a Swiss Army knife out of his front pocket and opened up blade. Lyn knew a lot of guys who carried those; they were almost never sharp. *I might as well gnaw through the strings.*

"Good. I have your attention. Now what makes you so sure she won't shoot at you?"

"I don't know." *Standing there in front of the windows unwinding the shade pulls like it's a regular old sunny morning. Of course she's going to shoot me.*

"What made you say 'yes' in the first place?"

"She used to like me. I'm nice to her."

Beau called out, "This is why I told you not to serve her! She's a nutcase!"

Lyn shot an angry look at Beau, though he couldn't see it from his safe spot behind the counter. The man underneath the booth tried to refocus her attention. "Hey. *Hey!* Ignore him. You don't think she likes you anymore?"

"I don't know." She thought about Joanie's face earlier that morning. *Was there anything in how she looked or what she did that said she was going to go on a killing rampage?* Lyn couldn't think of a single sign that Joanie had given, and that scared her more than she had been since the shooting started. If Joanie had been planning on killing her when she walked into the restaurant, she certainly didn't show it. "I'm here, right?" she finally said.

"Do you think she'll at least hesitate if you're the one in her sights?"

"M-maybe. She already didn't shoot me once when she had the chance."

"Okay. That's good. Do you think maybe she'll wait long enough for you to run behind the wall over there?"

"Dad, what are you doing?" the boy asked.

"Shh." The man put his free hand on his son's knee. His son grabbed it and held on. "Well? You up for a sprint?"

"I don't understand. You can't get all of the blinds," Lyn said.

"Neither can you with your plan. But I'm assuming that since she hasn't come in here to get us, she's found a roost somewhere out there to wait for us to poke our heads up, right?"

"It's her house across the street."

"You're kidding."

"I wish," she said. The man's face went slack for a second before he composed himself again. Whoever he was, to Lyn he seemed cool under pressure. Talking to him was making her feel a tiny bit better. Still, she wanted to crawl under the table with him and his son and wait the day out instead of finishing the task in front of her.

"Okay. So she's got a secure vantage point from which to see everything and she knows the layout of the place because she's the neighbor. I was trying to think how to get to our car without being seen, but I can't come up with a way to do it without getting blown away, I guess." He slumped beneath the booth and pulled his son close. "I'm officially out of ideas."

"There's still the blinds," Lyn said. "If we both jump up to cut them at the same time then she can't see anywhere inside and the whole place is ours. We can lock up and try to figure something else out."

"She might not shoot you, but I'm still presumably a target. We need a distraction."

"We've got my manager, Beau."

"The hell you do!" Beau answered.

"Listen. She could have killed you too when you came out that door, but she didn't," Lyn said. "If you stand up, she'll wait a second because she's, like, saving you for last or something. You stand for one second, get her attention, and then drop down and we'll cut the cords."

"Forget it."

"I crawled out here through glass, you motherfucker! You stand up when I tell you or I will crawl over there and hold you up for her!" Lyn clapped a hand over her mouth, as shocked that she'd stood up to Beau as she was by the language she used to do it.

"It's a good idea," the man agreed. If she really is trying to punish you, Beau, you're our best bet. At least if this works, I can move around and help take a look at the woman behind the counter and," he said to Lyn, "at your cuts."

"And what do you think you're going to do when you 'take a look'?"

"I'm a doctor; I can help. But not while we're being shot at."

"The blinds'll drop if we cut 'em quick," Lyn said.

"Except you don't have a knife. Unless there's one I can't see hidden in that apron."

"I don't have one." Lyn said.

The man twisted around, contorting so he could reach up between the booth seat and the edge of the table without exposing himself. "Got it!" He sat down with a steak knife in his hand. "Feeling pretty lucky I ordered the steak and eggs," he said, smiling. He wiped the grease coating the knife off on his pants and lightly tossed the knife toward Lyn, handle first. It clattered to a stop in the glass a few feet in front of her. She stretched as far as she could and teased it over with the tips of her fingers.

"Sorry about the toss."

"S'okay." She knelt there, staring at her blurry reflection in the still greasy knife.

"What's the matter?"

"I don't think I can do it."

"Did you think you could crawl through glass?" he asked.

"No."

The man smiled at her. Not a forced smile, but a real one, like he saw something in Lyn that impressed him. "But there you are." Whether she wanted to or not, she was doing what needed to be done. No wishing or shitting. She used her hands to make something happen.

"Now Beau," he called out. "I want you to get onto your feet, but stay crouched down. Don't stand up yet! Stay squatting. I'm going to count to three. On three—like this, one, two, GO! On three, you're going to pop up like whack-a-mole." He turned to Lyn. "You—what's your name?"

"L-Lyn."

"All right, Lyn. I'm Neil. Neil Tate. And this is my son, Hunter. We're pleased to meet you."

"Okay. Me too, I guess." She was actually very relieved to meet them. When they'd first come in the restaurant she had tried to serve them as quickly as she could and get them on their way, afraid that one of the local bigots might cause trouble for a pair of black guys. Now, she felt ashamed for not treating them more politely. That was life in Post-Racial America.

"When Beau creates the diversion, we're going to jump up and go for those cords." He pointed his pocketknife at the lines. "Beau! Wave your arms or something while you're up, okay? Try to draw her attention. But don't linger!"

"Go to Hell!"

"Okay." Lyn sniffled and wiped at her eyes with the backs of her hands. She needed clear vision to avoid tripping over the booth bench and landing in a pile of glass.

"When the blinds come down, Lyn, you head for cover behind that brick wall by the door. Sound like a plan?"

It sounded like a better plan than the one she had come up with. At least she was *sharing* the risk now. "I suppose," she agreed. Lyn didn't think she'd ordinarily bet her life against who someone hated more, her or Beau, but it was too late to argue. She was stuck in the middle of a field of glass, and she'd much rather return to the lunch counter on her feet than on her knees.

"Now, get up, but stay low."

"Dad?"

"Hunter, we don't have time. If Lyn's legs cramp, she won't be able to jump up and then we'll lose our chance."

"But Dad."

"Stop it." The man looked sternly at his son. "This is who we are. What do we do when we are able?"

"We help people," the teen said in a resigned tone that sounded it had been a mantra of theirs for years.

"And are we in a position to help *these* people?"

"No. Maybe. I don't know." The boy withdrew his hand from his father's. He knew what had to be done.

"Well, 'maybe' is good enough for me. We won't know until we try. Now, if this doesn't work, I want you to wait here for the police. Don't move."

"But you said…"

"If this doesn't work, then your first answer was the right one," Neil said. He turned his attention toward Lyn. "Are you ready?"

"Yes sir," she said.

"One." Neil shifted under the table into a position ready to scuttle out.

Hunter tried to make himself small, crunching up and wrapping his arms around his legs.

"Dad."

"Two."

"Be careful."

Lyn held her breath waiting for Neil Tate to say 'three.' She wasn't sure it was in her to sprint toward the windows like he said; it had taken everything in her to crawl to where she was, and her hands and legs hurt so badly. *You just have to. You don't have any choice. Neil's going to jump up on 'three' and if you don't do the same, Joanie's going to murder him and it'll be like you murdered him because you were too chickenshit to go.*

"THREE!"

Lyn sprang up and, as Neil feared, her leg cramped and she almost fell over. Nevertheless, she staggered as quickly as she could into the booth and started sawing away at the cords with her slippery steak knife. She heard the first shot and felt the bullet streak by her face at the same time, the hot breeze along her cheekbone making her lurch back involuntarily. The curtains dropped and she threw herself toward the door, clutching at the stinging line on the side of her face. She heard the other curtains drop and a second shot followed by a howl of pain from Neil and the sound of his heavy body hitting the floor.

"DAD!"

"Stay put!" Neil shouted. His voice was tight with pain and he clutched his thigh while he writhed on the killing floor. Another shot ripped through the blinds and the coffee pot on the warmer behind the counter exploded. The redhead shrieked and Beau and Luis shouted.

"Are you okay?" Lyn shouted over them.

"Yeah. It's okay, it's okay." The groan of pain that escaped in between sentences said otherwise. "It's my thigh. And I fell in the fucking glass!"

"Dad."

"It's okay, Hunter. Stay put. We've almost got it." Two more shots pierced through the rattan blinds sending small shafts of light peeking through, but didn't tear them down.

"I can come get you," Lyn shouted.

"Stay where you are! She's already missed you once. But I think your theory about her liking you has been disproved."

"Dad!"

"Hunter, what?"

"That guy never got up."

PART THREE: EVERYBODY PAYS

14 July 2013 — 1527 hrs

The pickup truck rumbled up the highway, its Hemi engine roaring as Andy Johnston gave it more gas to get up the steep grade. The truck was his baby. A gift from his father on his sixteenth birthday, he poured every cent he had into making it his dream ride. His first investment had been a rear window decal of an angry-looking eagle with stars and stripes wings. Since then, he'd added lifts, a roll bar with KC lights along the top, a chrome grille guard, and a net replacement for the tailgate to reduce wind drag. As soon as his summer job ended, he intended to spend the money he'd saved installing a new chrome exhaust system. He was close to his goal, but not quite there yet since he always set aside a little of his earnings for weed.

"Why do we have to come all the way out here, Andy? That dude who lives on Third is always holding. We could go see him." Andy shot his friend, Daniel, a look that said, *thanks for playing.* Still, he took the opportunity to explain himself for the benefit of the girls in the back of the extended cab.

"I don't care what Bryan's got. His shit is always weak, dude. I called Leonard last night and he said he's got the real sticky icky, but it's selling out fast. If we want to cop, we have to do it today."

"All I'm saying, man, is that an hour and a half drive for weed is—" Andy punched Daniel in the shoulder a little harder than a simple good-natured poke.

"Who said you were going to get any, anyway? This score is for me and the ladies, am I right?" Andy held up his hand for the girls to slap. His girlfriend, Paula, obliged, but Raylynne kept staring out the window. "Aw, don't pout, Rayray. If you're good, I'll take your boyfriend to get his vagina waxed after we spark up." Andy laughed too hard to notice that no one else thought the joke was funny.

"Why does Leonard sell all the way out here? Doesn't he, like... live in town?" Raylynne asked.

"Yeah, but it's like drive-through service. And since we're way outside of town, he doesn't have to worry about the cops jacking his shit up at home." Andy actually didn't enjoy making the long drive, but Leonard had the best dope in the panhandle. He also played up their friendship. Leonard usually only said one or two words to him when he copped: price and thanks. But Andy wanted the others to think that he had a personal relationship with the guy. He thought it added to his "cred."

Andy craned his head over his shoulder as they passed a blur that, for a second, looked like a set of prize antlers moving through the woods. *Probably just branches blowing in the wind.* He wished he had seen them through the scope on his thirty-aught, though.

Daniel rubbed his sore shoulder. "It's still a far way to go for a dime. Just sayin'."

"Wait 'til to you get a taste." Andy pulled around the bend and the neon sign advertising *Your Mountain Home Kitchen* came into view in the distance. At the same time, another car appeared in the rear view mirror. "Fuck! Shit!"

"What's the problem, Andy?"

"Cop."

1527 hrs

Neil sat on the dining room chair with his bandaged leg extended straight out. It hurt like hell, but the bullet had passed straight through the muscle. While it was far from the worst that could have happened to him, he was wasn't walking it off. And he could still bleed to death. The wound bled badly, but the makeshift tourniquet was stanching the flow, slowing the blood loss to a trickle. A very serious trickle that would have a definite effect on his ability to function, or even survive, if it was left too long.

Lyn sat in front of him on another dining chair as he finished picking pieces of glass out of her knees. He dabbed her wounds with alcohol-soaked *Q-tips* taken from the restaurant's first aid kit as she gritted her teeth. She stared straight at him with glassy blue eyes, trying not to look at his work. The two-inch line of burned flesh below her left eye, where the bullet had grazed her face, would likely scar.

She hadn't seemed it when he'd first seen her behind the hostess counter, but the girl was tough.

The glass embedded in his own back was killing him, but he needed to get her fixed up first. He was coming to realize she was the only certain ally he and his son had if they wanted to get out of the restaurant alive. Beau stood, watching him work, not offering help. Although Neil figured that Beau was likely shell-shocked from the assault, and could hardly be blamed for his cowardice, he intended to blame him fully when they were free and clear of the restaurant.

"There. That's it." He dropped the last piece of glass onto the plate that Hunter held out. Blossoms and trails of thin pink blood coated the dish like a raspberry drizzle over dessert. "You're lucky. No debilitating damage that I can see from eyeballing it and you've got full range of motion. You keep these clean and cared for and..." He meant to say, "and you'll be fine." The fact that none of them would be fine if the shooter found another way to come at them gave him pause. "And they won't get infected," he finished instead.

"Thank you," she said.

He grimaced as he straightened up and accidentally bumped against the back of the chair. Trying to hide the pain, he wiped Lyn's blood off of his hands onto his jeans. He looked at the redhead still sitting with her back to the counter cradling her lover's head in her lap. She ran her hands over the other woman's short hair, smoothing it one way and then another while she rocked back and forth, singing softly. After he'd stabilized his bleeding and made sure his son was all right, he'd gone to see if there was anything he could do to help the woman. There wasn't. The assassin's bullet had killed her instantly. The redhead's emotional wounds, by the same token, were far beyond his skills. She stared back at him and he felt the sting of his impotence.

"What's your name?" he asked.

"Carol," she said.

"What's hers?"

The woman stared into her lap and whispered, "Sylvia."

"I'm sorry." Feeling helpless and angry at his inability to bring back the dead or soothe the trauma of watching her lover die, he left her to her grief.

Neil stripped the field dressing off of the wound to his thigh. Both his jeans and the belt he'd wrapped around the holes in his leg were saturated with blood. The bullet penetrated the vastus lateralis muscle to the outside of his femur before exiting through the biceps femoris in the back. Through and through. He was lucky. If the shot had penetrated on the other side of the bone and severed his femoral artery, he could have bled out in minutes. If it had shattered the bone, he'd be worse than useless—unable to stand or crawl or even cope with the pain without opiates. Still, the first aid kit wasn't going to cut it. He needed to get to a hospital before he got an infection. Even if he didn't bleed out, he could still die from septicemia. Sucking in a long breath through his teeth in anticipation of the pain, he unbuttoned his jeans so he could get a closer look at the hole in his leg.

"Hey there. You just wait a minute," Beau said, finally breaking his silence.

"You have something to say to me, boy?" Pain, frustration, and fear had robbed Neil of whatever Zen calm he might have otherwise possessed. He stared hard at the man in the ridiculous western suit. Despite wearing boots with extra high heels, Neil towered over him. Still, the manager clearly wasn't used to people standing up to him. For a moment, it seemed like he wanted to bark back. Instead, he glared at Neil. "I didn't think so." Neil stood on his good leg, leaning on Lyn for support and pulled his pants down to his knees. "I'll have plenty to say to you as soon as I'm done here. Until then, you're better off sitting where you were."

"I don't like being spoken to like that."

"Get used to it. I don't like counting on someone to have my back and being let down. Believe me that we're going to have that out, too. But not until we all get out of here. Before then, we're working together. You feel me?"

Beau didn't throw his hand into the circle and swear to follow Neil's lead. He sat quietly and watched Neil clean his wound. Neil was sure that any action he suggested would have to be couched in a what's-in-it-for-Beau rationale.

"Yo, man, what do you expect?" the busboy weighed in. "You think he's going to jump up and catch a bullet when you say? Look what happened to you." Luis took a step forward, chest puffed out, pointing at his thigh accusingly. Neil was used to being the physician in charge in his Emergency Department. If anyone had a question about an order he gave, they were welcome to bring it up at the review meeting. Not before. He felt like he was losing whatever semblance of that control he'd taken by standing there with his pants down, but there was no other way to properly assess the wound.

"No one's talking to you, son. Not yet."

"I ain't your fuckin' son." Luis stepped forward again and made a gesture as though he were going to push Neil. Hunter slid in between them, spun Luis around and wrapped his arms around the busboy's throat in a choke hold. He locked one hand into the crook of his elbow and applied pressure with the fist of his other hand, pressing it into the crook of the other elbow. Luis' eyes bugged out as he tried to catch an impossible breath in the locked rear naked choke.

"Hunter?"

"Yeah, pop?" Although Luis was struggling and clawing at Hunter's thin but sinewy arms, he showed no outward sign of having to exert himself to hold the larger boy in place.

"Let him down." Hunter did as he was told, dropping Luis gracelessly to his knees. The busboy held his throat, gasping for air. "You're dead," he threatened. "Both of you, faggots."

"We're all dead we if don't work together," Lyn said.

"He suckered me from behind like a little puss—"

"He'll be happy to give you another shot head-on when we're out of this shit. But until then, Lyn's right. We're on the same team whether we like it or not. Fighting each other is just giving that woman out there what she needs to take us all down."

"Yeah, what's that?" Luis said.

"Time to get around our expert defenses," Neil said, pointing toward the blinds. "I understand none of us is feeling at our best right now. But we've got to get ourselves working together tout suite. That means setting aside differences and grudges. Are we all on the same page?"

Luis stepped away and gave Hunter one last hard stare. "Whatever, man."

Lyn tried to put a reassuring hand on Luis' shoulder, saying, "It'll be okay." The busboy batted her arm away and sat behind the counter. He began pulling at his fingers, popping each knuckle in turn.

Neil did his best to re-dress the wound using a med kit designed for treating kitchen grease burns and minor steak knife cuts. Lyn returned to his side and handed him a sterile gauze pad without being asked. She helped him tape it to his leg while he held it in place. She was a little clumsy, due to her bandaged hands, but did a good job nonetheless. He pulled his pants up and used the Swiss Army knife to hack the sleeve off Hunter's hoodie. He tied the make-shift tourniquet above the wounds and cinched it with a butter knife he could twist to periodically loosen and retighten it. Pain lanced up and down from his hip to his ankle and he felt faint.

Jesus, I've lost a lot of blood. He couldn't vocalize his concern; Hunter needed him to be strong.

Sitting backward in the chair, he carefully unbuttoned and stripped off his shirt. "How's it look, Lyn? Is there a lot of glass?" Although she was a waitress, from the last fifteen minutes of their shared experience he reckoned that she'd be up to the task of helping him remove whatever was stuck back there. She shook her head and set about the task of pulling pieces of shattered window out of his skin. He heard her breath quicken, but otherwise she gave no sign that the job was beyond her capabilities. He gritted his teeth and wished for a couple of Percocet or Vicodin.

"It's time we put our respective self-interests aside and start figuring out a way for us all to get out of here. Where's the rear exit?"

"It's through those swinging doors," Lyn offered. "There's another way out on the other side of the building by the bathrooms, but neither one goes anywhere."

"What do you mean?"

"There's a gravel lot in the back where we keep the dumpster, but that's it. Past that, it's the mountain."

A look of devastation flickered across Neil's face. He'd been counting on a service road at least. Now, he didn't know what to do. "Can someone climb down the hillside and go for help?"

"Not unless you'd rather commit suicide than get shot," Beau chimed in. "This used to be mountainside. Back when they made the highway, they carved out this plot for a scenic overlook or something. All the loose rock they blasted out got thrown down the side of the mountain. It's a steep scree slope with dense forest at the bottom. If you don't break your neck going down, without a GPS you'll get lost during the forty-mile hike into town."

"So we're stuck here for the duration?"

"Looks like it," Beau said.

Neil closed his eyes and sighed. He sat still for a minute trying to clear his muddy thoughts, but was having a hard time. He wanted to lie down and go to sleep. *That means you've probably already lost too much blood.*

"Two things. First, we need to shut off the sign outside," he said. "Let people know the place is closed before the dinner rush."

"And second?"

"We need to find a way to get word out. Let the world know we're up here."

"Who put you in charge?" Luis asked, still cracking his knuckles.

Neil pointed at the windows. "She did."

1530 hrs

"Is he pulling us over?" Daniel asked Andy as he continued to watch the police car following them up the highway in the rear view mirror.

"Nuh uh."

"Then be cool. We haven't scored yet. We can turn around and get some weed from Bryan." Daniel flinched, waiting for the second punch to his bruised arm. It didn't come. Instead Andy kept his hands on the wheel and his speed at fifty-five.

"Fuckin' cops, man. If we turn around, they'll know we ain't up here to buy fuckin' lunch. We're going in. You guys are going to get something to eat and I'll meet Leonard in the back. Cops'll never know what's going on if you play it cool."

"That sounds good," Paula said. "I'm hungry."

Daniel didn't reply. He had brought enough money to contribute to grass and gas. Lunch was going to really stretch him thin. He looked at his girlfriend in the backseat, about to ask if she'd brought any extra cash. His question was cut short by Andy's heavy hand thumping the middle of his chest.

"Don't *look*, dude!"

"I was gonna say something to Raylynne," he gasped. The blow had knocked the breath out of him, along with his last shred of patience. If they ran into anyone he knew at the restaurant, he was definitely hitching a ride home with them, weed or no weed.

"Just play it cool and we'll all get baked and mellow out. I promise."

Daniel sighed and turned around in his seat, nodding. Andy had a way of making it seem like no matter how big a jerk he was at that moment, it was all going to be okay in the end. And it always did because he was Andrew Johnston and everybody loves Andrew Johnston.

Andy slowed and pulled the truck into the restaurant lot, parking as close to the side of the building as he could. The Sheriff's vehicle turned the opposite direction and pulled into the driveway across the street. "See? Nothing to worry about. He's not even coming in here."

"Dude, are they even open?" Daniel pointed at the blinds.

"Fuckin' better be. Leonard told me he was working until late." Andy leaned over and looked up. "Sign's on. They're open." He opened his door and began sliding out, lighting a cigarette before his feet could hit the gravel. "Let's go."

"I think I'd rather wait here," Raylynne said.

"Me too," Daniel agreed.

"Bullshit. Get out of the truck and come inside. You're getting something to eat. Remember the plan?"

"The 'plan' was for when that cop was up our ass. But you said he—"

Andy spun around on his boot heel and glared into the truck. "Jesus, man. Why are you being such a pussy?"

Daniel held out the twenty he was contributing. "Go get your weed. We'll wait here. Raylynne, you got yours?"

"Sure, whatever." She didn't care about the pot; she'd visited her mother's medicine cabinet to satisfactory end before they even left town. She passed her bill to Daniel.

Andy leaned into the truck and grabbed the twenties. Stepping back, he winked and took a drag from his cigarette. It was going to work out his way in the end. Like it always did.

He opened his mouth to say something, but the crack echoing through the air cut him off. He heard a loud plonk of a bullet impacting against the open driver's side door. Andy looked over to inspect the hole that had appeared in his door. "The fuck?" The second round caught him in the side. He dropped to his knees, head bouncing off the door before he slumped down in the gravel, too breathless to scream or even to choke on the blood replacing the smoke in his lungs.

The girls in the back screamed for him.

Daniel climbed over the stick shift and onto the driver's seat as another shot ripped through the rear window, through the passenger headrest, and spider-webbed the windshield. Daniel fumbled with the ignition, looking over his shoulder. *What the fuck?* Why *is that cop shooting at us?* He couldn't see anything. At least the American eagle decal held the window together. The shooter still couldn't see inside.

He tried the ignition again, but it didn't budge. Andy's keys lay outside in the gravel where he'd dropped them. Another shot slammed into the back of the truck and Daniel heard Paula grunt and gasp. For the first time, he noticed that the windows in front of the hanging restaurant blinds were either missing or had holes in them. Bullet holes. He decided he couldn't spend time taking in the scenery while Raylynne screamed her head off and Paula... he didn't want to acknowledge what the noises Paula was making meant. He needed to get them out of there.

He clenched his fists and took a second to steel up his nerve before pitching himself out of the car. Lurching onto his hands and knees, the parking lot gravel dug painfully into his left palm. His other hand landed squarely in a slippery mess. The stench of it reminded him of cleaning a deer he'd accidentally gut shot. The animal had been squarely in his sight, but it had stepped forward as he took the shot. His dad had been furious that they'd had to track the suffering animal for over a mile through the woods and as punishment made him clean it entirely on his own. It was the last time he'd been hunting with his old man. *If I get out of this, I swear I'll visit Gramma and Grampa every single day. I'll go hunting with my dad. I'll go to church, God, I swear.*

Pulling his hand away he got a good look at the hole in Andy's stomach, pumping out blood and reeking of punctured intestine. He fumbled beside his friend's body for the keys. One jabbed into his raw palm making him yelp. Grabbing them, he tried his best to pop up and leap for the truck. A bullet hit the gravel where he'd been kneeling and kicked dirt and rocks into his face.

He sputtered and fell to his stomach, lacing his hands around the back of his head in surrender. "Shit man, don't shoot! We didn't do anything! Don't fuckin' kill us!"

"Jesus, kid! Head for the door!"

Daniel heard the sound of a pistol firing rapidly and then another shot from the monster rifle that was no thirty-aught. He couldn't tell where the voice had come from over the shooting, but he couldn't listen to it and leave Raylynne in the truck by herself. He did his best to jump up like before, but two hard falls on the ground had knocked the wind out of him. Hands gripped him under his armpits and hauled him up. Raylynne was out of the truck and dragging him to the door. He protested. "We got to get Paula to the hospital. I got the keys!"

"Paula's dead!" she shouted. Daniel saw the cop pulling himself beneath their pickup truck, leaving a trail of blood in the gravel.

"Inside! Get inside!" the cop yelled.

Daniel fell over the corpses blocking the door. He shrieked. A hand from inside the restaurant grabbed his belt and pulled him over the bodies as another shot took out the front door, spraying them with glass.

"CHRIST!"

"Get away from the door!" someone cried from behind the lunch counter. "She can still see you there!"

Lyn grabbed at the girl and swung her around behind the wall, knocking over the gumball machine. Unlike everything else in the restaurant, it didn't break. Daniel scrambled into the restaurant heading for the dining area. Lyn grabbed him by the belt again and pulled hard, barely stopping him. "Not that way," she hissed.

Neil shouted over his shoulder, "Luis, you and Hunter get the lights in the back." The boy ran off through the kitchen doors, Luis lagging behind. "Lyn, get these two behind the counter." From his seat he waved the trio toward him. "Is there anybody else out there?"

Daniel stuttered, but couldn't get an answer out. Neil gave him a quick once-over, looking for wounds. Although one hand was elbow deep in blood, the boy had made it in with just a little road rash on his palms. Both kids were shaken nearly to the point of catatonia. He grabbed Daniel's face and looked him hard in the eyes. "I said, is there anybody else out there?"

"My friends are... are dead. A c-cop. He killed..."

"There's a policeman outside?" Beau asked.

Daniel nodded but didn't say more.

Another bullet ripped through the blinds, slamming through the lunch counter spraying shards of shattered dinner plates on the survivors. "It's not safe here. We've got to get into the back," Lyn said. The counter wasn't any better protection than the blinds. Joanie couldn't see through them, but they didn't stop her bullets. If she stepped up her assault they were still too exposed. Lyn didn't want to think about what Joanie's next step would be, but she was pretty certain that this wasn't all she had planned.

Beau was frozen in place below the order window. "The kid says there's a cop out there."

"If he's not in here with us, he's dead," Lyn said. "Come on. Help me." She tried to lift Neil from his seat with little success. Despite his natural complexion, the doctor was growing dangerously pale and could barely hang on to her.

"He c-crawled under Andy's t-t-truck." Raylynne stuttered as she ducked under Neil's other arm to help.

Lyn lacked faith that whoever else had shown up outside was their savior. But there was one thing that held a glimmer of hope. *Even if he's dead, there's a police car out there with a radio and probably a gun.*

"He shot my friends. He killed them," Daniel said.

"He didn't shoot your friends."

Beau squinted, as if narrowing his eyes would allow him to see around the corner without leaning. "If there's a cop out there, he'll radio for help. We just need to hang on until the cavalry arrives."

"If he got shot, he's not sending for backup. He's fucking dead," Lyn said. "We gotta get in the back. Now!" She kicked open the swinging door and lurched through with Neil hanging off her shoulder. Raylynne wasn't much help, but she afforded Neil the extra balance he needed to hobble along on his good leg. Lyn set him on the floor as gently as she could and limped to the wall by the front window. There was no way to see outside without climbing into a booth. Though the blinds were down, she was pretty sure that if she got too close to them, Joanie would be able to see her silhouette. And being just a silhouette would mean whatever mercy Joanie had felt for her so far would be absent. Still, she wanted to see if it was possible to get into that police car.

"What are you doing?" Neil called out.

"Stay there. I'm taking a look."

"Let's wait for backup," Beau answered. "The police always radio in their position. When he doesn't respond, they'll send others."

"Just help get Carol into the back! I'll be right there!" Lyn wanted desperately for there to be a running police car waiting right outside the front doors. She fantasized that she could make a dash for it. Forget about the rips and tears in her knees and shins that made it uncomfortable to walk, let alone run—she knew she could run if she had to, jump inside, and be halfway to Mercy Lake before Joanie got a bead on her.

It's chickenshit to leave all these people. Except, if no one else knows what's going on, it's our only chance.

She slowly crawled into a booth, keeping her head low, and leaned around to look outside. She caught a glimpse of the back end of Andy Johnston's pickup and the blood trail leading to it, but couldn't see a police car or flashing lights. *Shit!* She looked behind her at Beau helping Carol off the floor. He glanced over his shoulder as he led the woman into the back. Lyn gave him a nod. He squinted at her as if he was suppressing a flinch, waiting to see if her head was going to pop like the bad tippers' had. When it didn't, he led Carol through the swinging doors.

Lyn faced the window. A light breeze moved the curtains slightly and she caught sight of Andy's body lying in the gravel. Beyond that was a dark blue figure she imagined was the cop. He wasn't moving either. *Well, that's it.*

She scanned the front of Joanie's house, searching for any sign of the shooter—her blond hair, a gun barrel. *It's too far away.* Lyn realized that Joanie was looking back at her through a scope. *That means she can probably see me pulling these—*

A bullet pounded through the window blind in front of her and she threw herself into the booth. Glass stabbed into her buttocks, but she didn't care.

She wasn't shot.

Ahead of her, in table five, was Bottomless Coke's dead body. She couldn't help but stare at him. He leaned out of the booth slightly, like a snapshot of a man getting up to head down the hall to take a pee after drinking six glasses of soda pop. Except he wasn't getting up. She figured, despite his gut holding him in place, gravity would eventually win out and he'd fall to the floor. Dead and alone. Whoever cared about him—a mother, a lover, even just a friend online—didn't have him to care about anymore.

Lyn felt a little crack growing inside of her. She sat waiting for her breathing to slow, crying into her hands. The tears and sweat soaking through the bandages stung her lacerated palms. *We're all going to die in here. We're going to die and no one is going to help us.*

She shuffled away from the booth. Leaning against the wall near the toppled gumball machine, she debated whether or not to head through the swinging doors into the back with the others. *I could wait things out here. No one needs me now. I got the windows closed and I've done all I can. I'm not a fantasy heroine and this isn't Brandybuck's.* All of a sudden, her sketchbook seemed like the most important thing in the world. If she could touch it, look at its pages, she could have a moment of normality before the inevitable happened and Joanie came striding through the front door to finish what she started. *It's nothing to anyone else, but it's mine. Everything I want to be is in that book. And when they find it on me, they'll know I wasn't just some skinny nobody working in a grease pit. I was more. I am more.*

The voice in her head took on a foreign character she wasn't used to. It was confident and convincing. *That book and everything in it is mine and nobody else's. Screw anybody who wants to take that away.*

She stood up straight and smoothed the front of her skirt and apron. She walked confidently over to the hostess station, unconcerned with whether or not she could be seen through the open front doors, bent down and retrieved the leather bound sketchbook from the drawer. Holding it was exactly what she had hoped it would be: a link to the moment before the world went to hell. She looked up and out at Joanie's house. *Will it hurt? Will I feel the bullet?* Like before, she couldn't see her killer, but she was certain Joanie could see her.

A movement in the line of trees bordering Joanie's property caught her eye. She watched as the bear the Colorado couple mentioned stood on its hind legs, with its head stuck in the low branches, and stared right at her. Shimmering in the leaves like a heat mirage, it didn't look like any bear she'd ever seen. It was at once familiar and alien in a terrible way. It looked like...

"Joanie!" Lyn's attention shifted at the sound of the cop shouting from underneath the truck. "Joanie, can you hear me?" he cried.

Lyn dropped behind the register stand and carefully peeked around. The bear thing was gone. *You're losing it. Keep it together. Stay in the really real world, okay?*

"Stay down!" she shouted. "Stay down. I'll get help!" Lyn tucked the book in her apron and slipped around the divider for the back.

Crashing through the swinging doors, she shouted, "He's alive. The policeman is..."

It took more than a moment for Lyn to process the scene in front of her. *Where did Luis get Jim's gun?* she thought, remembering her gun-nut ex-boyfriend who kept the same blocky looking pistol in the glove compartment of his pickup truck. He had a collection of guns that bordered on an arsenal, but that one was his favorite—it was the one they used in all the action movies he loved. A Glock. The unmistakable square design reminded her of the singular feature that had also sent her ex to the emergency room the time, trying to look cool, he'd shoved it in the back of his jeans: there was no outside safety switch to flick off like in the movies. If your finger was on the trigger, it was ready to fire. Or, if your pants caught on the trigger, it shot you in the ass. He'd been lucky he hadn't been trying to stuff it down the front of his jeans.

"I told you I would kill you, *maricón*," Luis said.

Raylynne and Carol shrieked, Beau might have shouted "don't" but Lyn couldn't hear over Hunter screaming, "DAD!" as he stood in front of his father in Luis' line of fire. Neil held up a weak hand like he might deflect the bullets.

"You *and* your faggot son!"

Beau hit the busboy in a low tackle, the two of them going down in a tangle. Luis fired, but the shot went stray, impacting somewhere in the kitchen. The gun slipped from his hand, clattering away. Luis and Beau struggled for a moment before Luis drove his knee fiercely into Beau's groin. Beau gagged and rolled onto his side, clutching his balls. Luis scrambled to his knees, feeling around for the gun.

Lyn pressed the barrel to the top of his head and asked, "Looking for this?" She could feel her pulse throbbing in her palm as she held onto the grip. Luis looked at her with a seething hatred and not an ounce of fear. She regretted her decision to get so close, but he didn't move. She held the gun as steady as she could, despite her ragged breath. Her grandfather had taught her how to handle guns even before she met Jim, and she remembered what he called "trigger discipline." *Always keep your finger outside of the guard until you are absolutely ready to fire, honey.*

"You can't do it," Luis taunted. "Do it, bitch. Pull the trigger."

Lyn dropped the gun away from Luis' head, moved her finger inside the guard and put a round in the floor in between his knees. He fell back, shrieking and cursing her in a flood of vulgarities uttered in two languages.

"Dad? Dad!" Hunter cried and held his father. The man who'd bandaged her wounds let loose a long wet sigh and slumped backward into the wall. If Lyn had thought she could attach her wagon to Neil's and ride to safety, she abandoned the thought. He was bleeding to death.

Beau sat on his knees looking at her in stunned silence. He raised his hands, palms out. Lyn eased her finger out of the trigger guard and lowered the gun.

"If anyone else thinks they're in charge, they're fucking wrong. From now on, all of you do what *I* say when I say it. Are we clear?" She pointed the gun at Luis' face; his stream of invective died and he lay there in silence. *"¿Claro?"* He glared at her. This time, however, there was plenty of fear in his eyes. Lyn fought the urge to murder him.

This is how Joanie feels.

1542 hrs

Bryce tried to get a look at Joanie's position from his hiding place under the kids' pickup truck without exposing too much of himself. If he could see her, he knew she could see him. When he'd imagined losing everything he loved because of his affair with Joanie, this wasn't how he'd pictured it. With his right hand—the one he could still feel—he popped the empty magazine out of his service piece, letting it drop in the gravel while he fished another off of his belt and reloaded. In all his years of service, he'd never fired his gun except on the range. Now he'd emptied an entire mag at his mistress' house. *This is crazy.* He fantasized for a second that her psychotic break would subside and he could go home to his family and forget that he'd been shot in the shoulder by a mad woman he was definitely through fucking.

Then he settled in for what was actually to come.

"Joanie! Don't fire. I want to talk to you." Nothing. He'd seen negotiators in movies calmly talk people down in all sorts of extreme no-win situations, but he simply could not think of a way to even open a line of dialogue with his girlfriend. He decided to keep shouting across the highway.

"I don't know what started this, but it can end right here. I already radioed in," he lied. "When I don't update that position in fifteen minutes, they'll send Chet up to look for me." Chet Carey had the next shift, but he wouldn't be coming to check on Bryce. He'd likely park his car at Morrell's Café on Main and Center and shoot the shit with the waitress at the counter until it was time for his lunch. Then he'd move to a booth and order. As far as a promise that the cavalry was coming went, it fell dead in the air as soon as he spoke it. "Oh, fuck it! Joanie! Say something, damn it!"

Still nothing. Hiding under a truck with six inch lifts gave him lots of room to move, but little cover, depending upon her angle. *I fired into the sitting room window by the front door, but she kept shooting. She's either above that in the bedroom, or below in the cellar.* He tried to recall the layout of a house. The first time they'd slept together, she'd taken him directly up to her bedroom. Afterward, he'd lingered a little in the kitchen, having a cup of coffee and pretending to ignore the guilt gnawing at him. Coming out of the house, his guilt took physical form when he ran into Brett Simmons from the Co-Op market leaving *Your Mountain Home Kitchen.* Brett insisted on pulling Bryce's ear in the parking lot, asking again and again what he was doing so far out of town. *It's not my business to say, Brett. The restaurant's part of the county, Brett. Making sure the taxpayers get their money's worth, Brett. Mind your own fucking business, Brett!* Since then, he'd insisted on meeting Joanie at Sleepy's Motel, far from anyone who might recognize either of them. Now, Bryce regretted not having a regular old reckless affair in the woman's house. Maybe once, she'd have asked him to go in the basement to look at a leaky pipe, or to move the washer, or any other mundane household task that would've let him know today where she might be sprawled out with a rifle.

You're running out of options, Bryce. Stay put and wait for the next set of customers to pull up and get blown away or get a move on.

There were people alive inside. He'd heard them shouting. Why wasn't he also hearing sirens? Why hadn't *they* called the police? Maybe they had and it was time to wait. *No way. You need to do something now.*

He twisted around to reach for the radio on his left hip. The effort sent pain arcing through his body. Despite it, he pulled the half-smashed radio free with his right hand. "Dispatch, this is Douglas. There's an officer-involved shooting at the *Your Mountain Home Kitchen* on Route 1A. I repeat, shooting in progress. Officer down!"

The radio crackled but he couldn't hear Carlotta respond. He shook the radio in frustration and heard loose pieces rattling around inside. The pain in his shoulder had overshadowed the ache in his hip from where he'd landed on the radio. *You broke it, you fat ass!* "Carlotta! Come in. Over!" More static. *I've got to get inside. They'll have a telephone inside and I can call for State Police backup if they haven't already.* He thought about his approach up the mountain. He'd have heard on the radio if there was a report of shooting at the restaurant. There had been nothing. *They should have called for help by now. Unless you took out the phones, Joanie.*

He clung to hope that getting out from under the truck was the first step toward defusing the whole situation. That is, until he heard gunshots inside the restaurant. He lay his head on the gravel and prayed to God for a plan to occur to him. It was the second time he'd asked for divine guidance in a week. The first answer he'd gotten was in the form of Cherie telling him to settle up his debts on the mountain.

Bryce was starting to think God was testing him. Or fucking with him.

1536 hrs

Joanie watched through her riflescope as Bryce struggled to crawl under the truck. *Why now? Why did you come to see me today? Why not yesterday when we still could have left together? I could have called the realtor and told him I want to sell the house after all. We could've taken the check, my lumps, and moved away together. We could've started over with the money someplace new.* She knew, though, that whatever Bryce had come by to do, it wasn't to whisk her away to some fantasyland where she was the happy little missus. He had kids. Worse than that, she was certain that he loved his wife. Joanie was a little red sports car he was joyriding in—trying to regain that nervous feeling in his guts he'd had when he was seventeen and took the keys to dad's Mustang.

He wasn't coming here to whisk me off my feet, she thought as she steadied the crosshairs on his exposed leg. *He was coming to tell me that it's over. It's over and I'm the other woman who gets to pack it in and start over from scratch while he goes back to his wife and kids and pretends that everything is like it was before. But nothing is ever like it was before. You make choices and then things go wrong and you get to live with the consequences for the rest of your life, Bryce. The things that you do—that other people do to you—last a lifetime and they never go away. They sit there like little demons and remind you how good it was before everyone started cutting little pieces off of your hide. They sit and laugh at all of your scars and make them itch and all you want to do is scratch until they bleed again.* Joanie slipped her finger inside the trigger guard, firing at the shadow behind the window blinds. It fell away. Not a hit, but a firm reminder.

This isn't over.

Bryce twisted around underneath the truck and his head came into view. She took aim. She wanted to scratch that itch so bad. She wanted to put everything behind her. But life was irreversible. *You can't take back what you've done. You can't take anything back ever. Everything you do has consequences. Caveat actor.*

He called out, begging her not to fire and to listen to him instead. She eased her finger off the trigger and watched her lover examine his shattered shoulder. She'd just wanted to kill the CB. He was facing her and the radio transmitter on his belt was behind him. She never wanted to kill him—or Lyn. Things just worked out that way.

She picked up the handgun lying next to her on the platform, and rolling onto her back away from the rifle, put the barrel in her mouth and asked for forgiveness. From whom it should come, she had no idea.

Then, she heard the shots and screams from inside the restaurant. *Everything you do has consequences.*

She pulled the gun from her mouth and lay for a while staring at the ceiling, thinking. About Bryce. About the past. About him riding her and what it had been like to be happy for a moment in time. She slipped her hand inside her pants and rubbed. She squinted her eyes shut harder and pictured him on his belly outside. She imagined him hurt and bleeding and paying for not calling her in five weeks. She imagined riding him and pushing his head into the gravel while his choking gasps kicked up rock dust.

She came. And the demons in her head laughed.

The one in the corner squirmed.

1612 hrs

"This is all your fault," Lyn accused Beau. "Yours and Adam's. You've been taunting her and pushing her and—"

"My fault? Are you out of your mind? She's the one killing people! Not me!" He wanted to get up to wash his hands after placing them on the greasy hallway floor, but didn't dare move unless he asked Lyn first. And there was no way he was asking permission from her to do anything. *I'd shit my pants on purpose first,* he thought.

"What about the Fourth of July? What was that?" He tried his best to look at her with a believable expression of astonishment. Two months earlier, he'd organized a Fourth of July celebration in the parking lot of the restaurant. A barbecue cookout, a DJ, and fireworks right over the restaurant. Shock and awe. The state cops came and shut them down as the display reached its crescendo. They threatened to arrest him but instead handed him a summons to appear in court for violating the drought emergency fireworks ban. Adam hired him a lawyer from Spokane and got the charges reduced. Beau plead guilty to disturbing the peace and received a fine which Adam paid. And afterward they both had a big laugh over a few beers while imagining Joanie cowering from the explosions. *I bet she was shivering in her G.I. Jane pee-jays whispering 'incoming,' all night.* Beau laughed and chugged another one of Adam's expensive microbrews that he thought tasted like bitter dog piss. But when Adam was buying, he never said no.

He deflected Lyn's accusation. "She's out there right now with a rifle and the target on *your* back and you're taking her side? The Fourth was just some good ol' American fun. If she can't take a joke—"

"Take a joke? You blasted Lee Greenwood at her windows and set off explosives over her house. She's a fucking combat veteran, Beau." Beau knew exactly what the sound of fireworks did to his own father: they sent him right into the jungle. He wondered where Joanie went—probably the desert somewhere.

"And do you think you're blameless?"

"I didn't do any—"

"You didn't call in sick on the Fourth," Beau said. "You didn't quit your job after the party. You showed up to work the day after, and the next day, and here you are today for a double. Do you think this place runs itself?"

"You're putting this on *me*?" Lyn stared at him with a new hardness that said that if Joanie didn't do the job, she might be perfectly happy to stand in for her. Behind her, Hunter glared at Beau and Luis with the same kind of intensity, only hotter. The lines were clearly drawn. Lyn, Hunter, and his old man, Neil, were on their side, and Beau had a wannabe gangsta busboy on his. In the middle were a couple of piss-pants kids from the high school and a near catatonic woman who couldn't stop crying. And the cook? Leonard was nowhere to be found.

Wouldn't be on my side anyway. The Chief always looked sweet on her. Chickenshit probably ran out after the first shot. Chickenshit or not, Beau wished that he'd followed Leonard instead of running in the direction of trouble. His only hope now was the cop outside. Law and order.

"Lyn, we can sit pointing fingers at each other for the rest of our lives, but it ain't going to get anybody unshot." He saw the hatred in her eyes intensify as he spoke. The boy behind her flinched. He needed to choose his words more carefully. "Look, we need to get out of here, and *then* there'll be all the time in the world for recriminations and saying sorry. Right now, Joanie has got us pinned down and you saw that she isn't letting anybody out of this. Shit, hon, she took a shot at you. So much for your theory that you're someone special."

"So what do you suggest? Maybe we can invite the DJ back up here and see if she's in the mood for a Labor Day party."

"What do you want from me? Do you want me to go outside and apologize? Do you think she'll pack up her toys and let us all go home if I do that?" Beau asked.

"Why don't you try it and see?" she said.

"Why don't we try working together like your boyfriend there says? We need to go through all the cell phones, like I thought of out there, and see if anybody can get a signal. Then, we need to see about getting that policeman in here with us. If she comes busting in through the front, I'd like to have someone who *doesn't* want me dead ready to defend us."

Lyn stood quietly for a moment. "I think you're right." She looked to Hunter, and said, "Sweetie, my phone is in locker number five around the corner. It's unlocked. Would you get it, please?" She turned to Beau. "Where's yours?"

"In the office, on my desk."

"Hunter, would you get that one too?"

She focused her attention on the kids huddled together under the sink. "What's your name?"

"Raylynne." She pronounced it "Raylin." Beau wondered if her parents had wanted a boy.

"My name's Lyn. You go by Ray or Lynne?"

"It's Raylynne."

"Whatever," she said. "Carol over there mentioned having a phone in her purse when this all started. I want you to go get it. It should be—"

"I ain't goin' out there. You can go fuck yourself." Lyn's eyes narrowed and Beau saw her face darken frighteningly. Raylynne stared at her with the kind of spoiled petulance he saw when he had his daughter over on the weekends. *She has no idea what she's bucking against.*

"Sweetie, *you* got a phone?" Lyn asked.

"Of course I do."

"Hand it over." Lyn held out her left hand. The girl looked like she might say something else, but changed her mind when her boyfriend held out his cell.

"I get to have it back, right?" he asked sheepishly.

"Of course you do, sweetie. Right away." She took the phones and stuffed them in her apron right next to the damned sketchbook he'd told her time and again to leave at home. She tossed her order tablet on the floor to make room in her pockets.

Beau considered tackling her like he'd done to Luis. *I saved her ass and she doesn't give a shit. I can take her down and get the gun while she's distracted and the jujitsu kid is out of the room. The only reason she's got it instead of a slug burning in her guts is because of me.*

Just then, Hunter came around the corner with the phones held out in front of him. He handed them to Lyn and then took his support position behind her again, glaring at Luis. Beau could see that murder was definitely on his mind and wondered what was holding him back. Was it Lyn or the influence of his father? If it was the latter, he could count on the kid acting rationally even though he had no reason to do so. If it was the former, well, all bets were off since Lyn seemed to be well past giving a shit at that moment.

"Everybody up. Let's all head to the office."

"Why?" Daniel asked. She gave him a sympathetic look.

"If Joanie comes through those doors behind me she's got us all dead to rights."

She pointed with the Glock toward the security mirror in the upper corner of the back room. Beau told them he'd installed it to keep staff from colliding with each other coming around the corner. He had no illusions that that anyone believed him. It was really so he could see if anyone was hanging out in the hallway taking a break.

"From the office we can keep an eye on the back door and the hall we're in now. Our chances are better if we can see her coming. Right?" She looked the question at her manager. If she was trying to regain his trust by appealing to him, it wasn't working. Instead, he felt manipulated and more unsettled knowing she was the one holding their only gun. Manipulative or not, however, she was right.

"You bet," he answered. Waiting out the siege in the hallway was like standing in the kill box hoping that the butcher had left to go to his retirement party.

"Help her," she said, gesturing at Carol with her empty hand. Beau got up and gently pulled the weeping woman to her feet. Daniel and Raylynne helped Neil. Luis tried to stare Lyn down. She wasn't having it. "You can wait here if you want," she said. "I can see you well enough in the mirror."

"*Puta.*"

"Come on, Luis. Quit goading her." Beau tried to put a friendly hand on the kid's shoulder, but the brat batted it away the way he had Lyn's.

"*¡Vete y chinga a tu madre!* It's *your* fault she's got my fucking gun."

"When you had the gun, you tried to kill me and my father! If she gave it to me I'd shoot you right in the face!" Lyn hugged Hunter. Luis jerked forward, but froze when she held up the Glock.

"On second thought, you're definitely staying in the hall," she said. "Consider yourself our canary in the coal mine. If Joanie comes through that door you can let us know by calling her a bunch of nasty shit in Spanish." She narrowed her eyes again and Beau felt that place in his guts go cold again. "I know what you're thinking," she continued. "Go to your office and get your rifle. I won't stop you."

"And if I come back for you with it?"

"Then I can tell the cops it was self-defense." She aimed the pistol between his eyes and slipped her finger inside the guard.

"What if I try to leave?"

"Be my guest. There are three exits. I'd just as soon you use the one in front."

1612 hrs

If he was correct in assuming that a position beneath the deck of Joanie's house gave her a better angle of attack, Bryce figured he could get out from under the truck and maybe halfway to the corner of the building without being seen from her vantage point across the highway. From there, he was exposed for ten or fifteen feet before he disappeared from view again. He holstered his pistol and began to pull himself forward. His left arm had gone pretty numb, except when he tried to move it—then it screamed pain. He let it drag beside him. For the first few feet he spent more time pulling gravel toward him than he did moving forward. He rolled onto his side and undid his utility belt. Rolling onto his stomach, he slipped it out from under him and draped it over his shoulders. He started forward again with slightly better result without his buckle digging into the dirt. Still, lacking the use of one arm meant he was inch-worming along more than crawling.

When he got to the wall he didn't wait to see if Joanie was going to take the shot, or even if he could get a glimpse of where she might be. He kept going, repeating his reasons for taking the risk: his wife and kids. *For Cherie. For Logan. For Annie. For Cherie. For Logan. For Annie.* Eventually, he reached the rear corner of the restaurant and let himself feel a tiny measure of relief as he rounded the corner.

He breathed deeply for the first time since pulling into Joanie's driveway. Although he prayed every week in church, he usually stuck to Our Fathers and Hail Marys. This time, he went off script.

"Dear Lord, thank you for looking after me in this moment of need. I'm not asking you to get me through this because I deserve to live, but because my family deserves to have the choice whether or not they want me around. Please, all I'm asking is for you to allow them that much." Mustering up the last of his energy, he got to his feet and shambled the rest of the way around back.

Leaning against the brick wall beside it, he banged on the door with the butt of his ruined radio. From inside he heard a startled yelp and a gunshot. A bullet hole opened in the door at chest level. "Cease fire! Sheriff's Department! Cease fire!" A moment later, the door opened a crack and a blood-stained girl in a pink waitress uniform poked her head outside.

"Did I get you?" she asked.

14 August 2009 — 1445 hrs – Iraq

Joanie lifted a box of medical supplies from the transport and carried it into the makeshift village hospital. The civilian contractor in the DeepWater tac gear leaned against a wall leering at her, not offering to help. She tried to put him out of her mind as she did her job. Technically, due to Pentagon rules, she was not allowed into a combat zone, but this area had been pacified and they were short hands for the mission. She'd volunteered to help deliver medicine for two reasons, the first being that helping people made her feel better about being so far from home, and second, it got her off base for a few hours. Anything that could break up the monotony of a typical day was welcome.

She walked past the merc, trying to avoid making eye contact without looking down. It was difficult. Her father had spent a lot of time encouraging her to look a man in the face. *If you want to be treated with respect, you got to demand it. Nobody is going to see you as an equal if you're always lookin' at your shoes.* This guy definitely did not see her as an equal, despite the Master Sergeant chevron sewn on her shoulder. The contractor exhaled between his teeth as she walked by, sounding like a leak in a gas line or a burning fuse. She thought he might've meant it to be a compliment. It didn't feel complimentary. "Why don't you make yourself useful," she said over her shoulder.

"It's below my pay grade, baby." He nodded his head at the M-24 rifle slung over her shoulder. "What are you supposed to be anyway?" She gritted her teeth and moved toward the hospital. Inside, the other members of the volunteer team were helping unpack boxes. There was a line of Arabic men in black robes eying the medics suspiciously. Some creep in Baghdad had started the rumor that American vaccination programs were actually a plot to infect and kill healthy Islamic men as a part of a religious crusade. Given how the men were looking at Airmen Morris and Jones, she guessed that the story had made it at least as far as this village. That was until she entered the house. Then their disapproving looks focused on her. Despite wearing her ABU utility cap, she figured her attire wasn't "modest" enough for them. She wondered if these were the kind of men who'd stone a girl to death for falling in love with a boy from the "wrong" tribe.

Don't judge, Jo. You're here to help.

Errol Normandy, her spotter partner, tapped her on the shoulder. "Don't let them get under your skin. They'll be happy as kids on Christmas as soon as they find out we've got penicillin to treat the clap." He winked. Although he normally knew exactly how to lighten her mood, today she wasn't feeling the *esprit de corps.* "What is it, Jo? These guys aren't going to do shit."

"It's not them. It's the DeepWater guys outside."

"Those dicks? Are they giving you a hard time?"

"No. Not really. They've just got creep turned up to eleven. I'm being oversensitive."

"You're never going to see them again. Let it go. Come on. I'll help you with the last of the boxes and then we'll go home and get a beer. What do you say?"

"Al Asad isn't home."

"It is until we're redeployed to Afghanistan."

"That's *definitely* not home!" Although she enjoyed the time away from base, she was glad this mission was nearly over. They'd delivered medicine and supplies to towns between Baghdad, Tikrit, and now Mosul. It would be nice to sleep in her own rack after the long drive back. She and Errol walked out to the transport and each grabbed a box. Her spotter turned around to give the contractor a hard stare when the first mortar hit.

Joanie dropped her box and took cover behind a low stone wall as another mortar exploded six or seven meters away. "They're getting a bead on the trucks," she shouted. Errol fumbled for his scope while the rest of the unit emerged from the hospital, found cover and returned fire, attempting to engage an invisible enemy bombarding them from somewhere in the nearby hills. She did her best to spot the mortar position through the scope of her rifle, but she couldn't get a fix on their position. The insurgents, on the other hand, were zeroing in on them.

Another shell exploded. More dust and debris floated in the hot air obscuring her vision. She saw the DeepWater guys running for cover while her team engaged. *Fuckin' figures!* As a counter-sniper, she was inclined to find a hide from which to locate the enemy team. Given what they were firing, however, she was already in as good a spot as any.

Someone beside her was shouting, "We're taking indirect!" as if no one else had noticed. While her fellow airmen were firing blindly at the side of the hill nearest them, Joanie and Errol were scanning for a target. Patient, but anxious to do their job. Over the chaos behind her, she heard the unfamiliar patois of whatever tribal language they spoke in the mountains. Some panicked airman shouted, "Jo! Behind you!" Joanie swung around in time to see a man racing out of the half destroyed house. Ahead of him ran a young girl, maybe eleven or twelve years old. Black hair spilled from her brightly colored headscarf. She was screaming and running right for Joanie's position. She reached out and gave the girl the hand sign she'd been taught meant 'stop' to these people. The girl ignored her.

Another mortar shell hit the wall behind the girl, blasting it to pieces and throwing the kid to the ground. Her shrieking stopped. The man pursuing her hit the dirt and covered his face as rocks and debris rained down on them. Joanie was half way to the girl before she even realized she'd left her position and cover. Errol shouted after her, but she couldn't hear. She took a knee beside the girl and rolled her onto her back. Half of her face was caved in. She was choking and sputtering muddied blood into Joanie's face as she stared helplessly into the girl's panicked eye.

The squad leader grabbed Joanie under her arms and pulled her away from the girl, shouting, "Leave her! Back to your position. Find that fuckin' mortar team and reduce the target!" The girl lay motionless in the dirt. The old man was retreating back into the house and the squad leader was on to someone else shouting something she couldn't make out. Joanie scrambled to her position beside Errol. "Got 'em," was all her friend said by way of greeting as she rested the barrel of her rifle on his shoulder. With Errol's directions, Joanie found the men bombarding them crouched halfway up the facing hill. They were loading another round. She focused in on the one about to drop a shell into the mortar tube. Correcting for drop using the mill dot relation etched into her scope lens, she confirmed her figures with her partner. Errol replied, "Send it." She fired. Through the scope she watched the man's chin tuck in like he'd been punched in the face.

"Right in the peach," she said, meaning she'd hit him right in the peach-sized medulla oblongata at the base of his brain. Perfect hit. Lights out. The fighter dropped the mortar shell on the ground instead of in the tube. While their spotter dropped his binoculars and fumbled around for the loose round, Joanie put another bullet in the brain of the insurgent aiming the mortar. He fell, knocking over the weapon. The fumbling man abandoned the round and ran behind the nearby rocks for cover.

The assault stopped; their squad leader ordered a cease-fire. Joanie waited patiently for the third man to poke his head up. Errol sat next to her quietly watching the scene.

"Anyone left, Sergeant Myer?"

Errol said, "Four meters right. Mooj behind the bush."

Joanie spotted the man trying to creep away on his belly. She adjusted her aim and squeezed the trigger. Her shot echoed in the fresh silence. "No one, sir."

Standing up, she waited to be reprimanded for breaking rank. Instead, Lieutenant Wilcox praised her and Errol for taking out the nest. Joanie looked over his shoulder at the girl lying in the dirt. The medic treating her got up and walked away to tend to other people who'd been hit by flying debris, leaving her body for her family to take away.

"You all right, Jo?" Errol asked.

Her attention was drawn from the girl to three of the black-clad DeepWater contractors emerging from a house far up the lane. "Sure. Let's finish up and get the hell out of here."

1820 hrs

"Those guys really got under your skin, didn't they?" Errol shouted over the rumble of the HMMVW troop carrier. Unlike in its civilian counterpart, noise dampening was not a feature that AM General added to the military line.

Joanie shook off her daze and focused on her partner. "What? Them? No. That's the job, right? Three shots, three *hajjis* down." Now that they were headed to Al Asad she had time to replay the firefight in her head. She had time to think about what it really meant to put three men's lights out.

"I don't mean the insurgents on the hill. I mean the fakes." Errol had heard an Australian soldier refer to armed civilian contractors as "fakes" and took to it like a heavy raindrop to gravity. She couldn't tell who he held in greater contempt, the insurgents or mercenaries. He was convinced that the presence of DeepWater Private Security Details anywhere in country doubled the risk that servicemen and women faced. The locals were becoming increasingly upset with the cowboy antics of mercs with loose supervision and little to no accountability. That frustration and distrust didn't help the rank and file accomplish the tasks they'd been sent to do.

"There was one who kept giving me the skunk-eye, you know?"

"Forget about it. Like I said, we'll never see them again. And if we do, they'll never see us." He patted his spotter's scope and winked again. "From a place you will not see..."

"Comes a sound PSD will not hear." She tightened her grip on her rifle and winked back.

The explosion outside rocked the vehicle. Joanie's head banged against the interior wall making her vision blur. The improvised "*hajji* armor" welded to the side of their Humvee held fast, protecting the occupants from the IED blast that crippled their vehicle, stopping them dead still. Errol was up and gripping her shoulders. "Jo? Jo! You with me?" The next hit sent him crashing to the floor of the truck. The last thing she saw before losing consciousness was the cab of the Humvee exploding in a ball of fire.

1940 hrs

Standing in the smoking aftermath, DeepWater PSD officer Jason Hess surveyed the damage. "Anyone alive up there?"

"No sir. Raghead RPGs got 'em all. How 'bout you? Find anybody?"

Hess bent down and felt Errol's throat for a pulse. It was faint, but there. "Yep! You guys better get over here." He leaned over and felt Joanie's throat next. Her pulse was stronger, but she was out as deeply as her spotter.

"Hey, lookit. It's that hot-shit sniper cooze," Podowski said, as he came around the truck.

"Yep," Hess said.

"Want I should call it in?"

Hess stood there for a long moment, weighing their options. He was sure that these troops had been able to radio their position before getting the shit blown out of them. If they hadn't, someone else was likely to come across them eventually and spread the word. In the meantime, he saw something he wanted. "When was the last time you saw a blond?"

"Shit, Hess. I dunno. Last time I was in the green zone, I guess."

"I mean one that couldn't say 'no.'"

"What are you thinking?"

"Get her in the truck."

"What about him?"

"He's on his own," Hess said.

Time unknown

Joanie swam in and out of consciousness. Awake one moment long enough to realize she hadn't been evaced to a hospital. At another, just long enough to catch a glint of gold dangling in front of her face.

And for one excruciatingly long time, she regretted not having been killed along with her best friend, Errol.

Time unknown

Laughter. "The carpet matches the drapes."

Time unknown

The pain came and went.

Time unknown

"Not so stuck-up now, you bitch. You cunt."

Time unknown

"Come on, man, you got firsties last time."

Time unknown

The humiliation was constant. Her hate grew until it filled all the tiny places inside her. It pumped with her blood while she slept.

Date and time unknown

Feeling groggy and disoriented, she lifted her head off of the stinking mattress. Her neck ached from craning it away from the nightmare of faces that leaned over her, panting their stinking breath at her. Her whole body ached in a way that made her wistful for the tortures of basic training. Whoever had used her last had left the LED lantern on. She got her first look at the room where she'd been held for the last... two days? Three? A week? She lay on a molding mattress on the floor inside of a narrow, corrugated commercial shipping can. The military used wider cans called "containerized housing units" instead of tents back on base, but this wasn't one of those. It was one used for shipping cargo. A few wooden pallets had been stacked in the corner to serve as a table. The lantern stood there along with a dirty plastic lunch tray—*have they been feeding me?*—and a taser. Except for the rust and dried up rat droppings, the rest of the can was empty.

She sat up. They'd dressed her in the same orange jumpsuit they used to clothe enemy combatants taken into custody. She wondered where the pointed vinyl hood was and why she wasn't wearing it. *Probably saving it for when they move me.* She had no illusions about how this encounter was going to end when the men holding her captive finished with her. *What is finished anyway? When I stop moving? When I stop breathing?* Whatever their idea of it was, when she was used up, they'd hood her, drag her out like a prisoner to a Humvee, drive her to the middle of the desert somewhere and dump her. If she was lucky, they'd bury her so she'd suffocate quickly instead of dying of heat stroke and dehydration. She wondered if she was still anywhere near her unit.

Hunger gnawed at her and she realized that if they had been drugging her, it was probably in the food. *If they were still feeding me, I wouldn't be waking up.* "Jesus!" she croaked. "How long have I been in here?" Her throat was dry and the painful attempt at speaking aloud emphasized her need for water. She crawled over to the pallets. A half empty water bottle rested on its side next to a tray smeared with the remnants of some MREs—Meals Ready to Eat: freeze-dried, high calorie nastiness. Although it was unbearably hot in the container and she desperately wanted the drink, she wasn't convinced that the water wasn't what they'd drugged her with instead of the food. *If you're getting out of here, you've got to be smarter than they are.* She crawled around behind the stack hoping to find something else to drink—an unopened bottle of spring water or a half empty beer can. Anything.

There was nothing.

She stood carefully, steadying herself against the wall. Tears clouded her eyes as the mere act of standing sent pain shooting from between her legs into her guts. She stumbled and caught herself on the unsteady table that threatened to collapse under her weight. The lantern fell over and rolled away. She stood as straight as she could and put her hand on the hot metal wall. Unable to lift her feet without excruciating pain, she shuffled toward the doors, the rough floor of the shipping container scratching her bare soles. Feeling her way along the wall, she moved toward a slender but dim vertical line of sunlight shining through the crack between the doors. *What if there's a guard?* She stumbled to the table and picked up the handheld stun gun. It was one of those small ones you can buy online to carry in your purse. She flicked the switch on and off shooting a brief bright blue arc of electricity between the two prongs at the end of the device. It had enough voltage to knock someone back or even down, but not unconscious. Still, it was better than nothing. *How many times did they use this on me?* She struggled to remember, but that was a detail that didn't rise out of the fog of her mind. Her whole body ached and it was impossible to locate a single point that felt like it had been electro-shocked as opposed to simply beaten or fucked.

Moving to the front of the can, she cradled the stun gun to her chest and pushed slowly against the doors with her shoulder. They bowed out slightly until the latches at the top and bottom of the portal caught and held, making a dull clanking sound. She wanted to weep, but held back the tears. *Escape first. You can have all the time in the world to panic as soon as you get yourself out of this. Toughen the fuck up!*

She looked around the can one last time for something that would help her escape. There were a few things that would be useful if she needed to walk through the desert—the blanket, the lantern—but little that would jimmy open a door or disarm a guard. Leaning back, she tried to batter the door with her body. Instead, she staggered back a hard step, nearly falling again. The jolt of pain in her abdomen made her vision dim. She doubled over and held her stomach for a long time, breathing through the agony, promising herself with every exhale that she'd kill the men who did this to her. She promised to kill them slowly, like they were doing to her. She imagined hurting them in intimate ways, channeling her anger to give her a boost of adrenaline sufficient to batter down doors made to hold shifting cargo whose weight was measured in tons.

She collected herself and tried once more, letting herself fall into the doors. The same pain welled up inside, but this time the doors clanged a little louder. They weren't going to open any time soon under her power. She hoped, however, that somebody might hear her—if the can wasn't sitting in the middle of the Arabian Desert. *And do what? Rescue me? Rape me again? Kill me?* She pointed the stun gun away from her body and jolted it again to reassure herself it was working. *Fuck 'em. Let 'em try. Hurry up, boys; come and get me.*

Rocking back and forth from foot to foot, she banged her shoulder against the door until exhaustion buckled her knees and she sat down hard. The ringing metal had echoed noisily in the can, but she had no idea how loud it was outside. *What if they did drop this can out in the desert? What if they are done with me and this is what they did? Leaving me to die locked in a shipping container that'll get buried in the next sand-storm?* She kicked at the doors despite the pain and screamed through her dry throat for help. Her hoarse voice barely echoed inside the steel coffin.

The blossoming flare of light made her fear for a moment they had thrown a grenade into the can. She shielded her stinging eyes, waiting for the fire and shrapnel to take her pain away. A man's voice called out from the blaze in a language she recognized but couldn't understand: Arabic. Suddenly there were hands on her and a dark shape took form as her eyes adjusted to the sunlight blinding her through the open doors.

She repeated the only two phrases she knew in Iraqi Arabic. "Hal tatakallamu alloghah alenjleziah? Ahtaju tabeeban!"

The man replied in halting, accented English, "Calm down. We will take you to hospital." He held out his hand in a gesture that she didn't understand. "May I have that?" he asked, pointing at the taser. She clutched it tighter to her chest. He appeared to give up and let her have her toy. "You will be all right," he said. "Don't shocking me." He was dressed in a long white dishdasha robe with a head veil tied with the egal headband. She had no idea what his clothes could tell her about who he was. But she hoped white meant he was a good guy.

The man picked her up and carried her out of her prison. As he walked toward a broken-down Toyota pickup truck loaded with scrap metal, they passed the bodies of the DeepWater contractors lying in bloody sand. A glint of gold on one corpse caught her eye. The dead man's cross pendant rested next to a seeping red bullet hole in his neck. She bucked a little in her rescuer's arms wanting to be let down. She wanted to make sure he was really dead. Kill him again. "It is all right," he assured her. "We go to hospital. You will be all right there."

She doubted that she would ever be all right again.

PART FOUR: LYN LOSES HER JOB

14 July 2013 — 1630 hrs

Although she'd nearly shot him with it, Bryce didn't ask the waitress, Lyn, for her gun. She scared him. In no little part, that was because her face was covered in drying blood like some kind of feral horror movie cannibal. But more than that, beneath the gore, she wore an expression he'd seen in the face of other people for whom *"from my cold dead hands,"* wasn't just a saying—and he'd already been shot once today. Although the look in her eyes clearly communicated that she was on the brink of coming undone, she was in charge and, so far, she'd kept this many people alive.

The others' attitudes ranged from pouting resentment to crippling fear to near catatonic shutdown. And then, there was the busboy. Bryce had seen his look before as well. He was looking for a way out—screw everyone else. Bryce needed an ally in the room, and Lyn looked like the only one ready and willing to get her hands dirty for someone other than herself. She'd helped the doctor patch up his shoulder and put it in a sling while everyone else sat in the back room waiting for Joanie to launch the next wave of her offensive. Right now, she was sitting against the wall with the doctor's kid, holding his hand and telling him that he and his father were going to be okay. In spite of the wild look in her eye and the easy trigger finger, Bryce found himself inclined to trust her.

Trying to steady his nerves, he pulled a pouch out of his breast pocket and awkwardly pinched out a wad of tobacco. He stuffed it between his lip and gums and tried focusing for a second on the sensation of the menthol and nicotine instead of the pain in his shoulder. He looked around for a cup to spit in. Though they were in a restaurant, he couldn't see one anywhere nearby, and resigned himself to swallowing the juice.

He checked his watch again. Even if his radio signal had gotten through—which he knew it hadn't—they still wouldn't be hearing sirens for a while. "There's nothing on the radio about this. Haven't any of you called for help?"

"Phones are out," Beau said.

"We were collecting cell phones when you got here," Lyn said. "There's shit for signal up here, but sometimes they work outside. I figured I could go out back and try."

"Why you?" Luis asked. "Who made you God?"

"I already answered that question." She patted the gun tucked into the front of her apron. "I already know you can't be trusted and I don't want to worry about what you're picking out from behind the propane shed to use to bash my head in."

"Propane shed?" Bryce said. "This place is fed by propane?"

"Did you see any solar panels out there?" Beau said. Bryce narrowed his eyes and gave him what his wife, Cherie, called 'Cop-face.' Beau buttoned down the sarcasm. "We got a propane tank on the side of the building."

"How big is it? How much does it hold?"

Beau rubbed his chin. "Hell if I know. A god damned lot'd be my guess."

"I need to see it."

"What for?"

Bryce didn't want vocalize his fear. He hoped that whatever had made Joanie want to go on a killing spree had been a spur of the moment thing and not a plan that took days or weeks of preparation. He took small comfort in the fact that the shed hadn't already exploded, but he'd come to know Joanie a little bit; she didn't go for a run without a plan. "I don't know yet. But it's better than sitting here waiting."

"Well, you can't anyhow," Beau said.

"Why not?"

"Two reasons. One, it's kept locked by the propane company. The only ones who have a key are the owner, Mr. Bischoff, and the guy who comes to fill the tank."

"How often do they come to fill it?"

"Couple, three times a month. On Thursdays, so we always have a full tank for the weekend."

"That's got to cost a fortune. How does this place turn a profit?"

Beau smirked. Bryce thought his teeth were weirdly straight and white, like a bad artist's depiction of perfect teeth instead of real ones. "This place ain't made a profit since it opened."

"What? Why stay open if you're losing money?" Lyn asked.

Beau nodded in the direction of Joanie's house. "Mr. Bischoff says so."

Bryce recalled lying in Joanie's bed after their first time together. He'd asked her why she moved into a house across the way from such an eyesore. She'd said it wasn't there when she bought it. Although they didn't talk much about her personal life, he read the papers. He knew she'd been fighting for at least two years to shutter *Your Mountain Home Kitchen*. She'd done everything she could to get the place closed, but Bischoff practically owned Boundary County politics. If he wanted something, he called up a friend who owed him a favor—and that meant practically any living official in the county, including the judge hearing the case. *The only person in the county who doesn't owe Adam a thing is probably Joanie. That's why he's doing this. And that's why she's doing what she's doing.*

"Adam says that we stay open until he gets the call that she's ready to sell," Beau added.

"We're only up here because the fucking boss wants to buy a house?" Lyn shouted. "How's that working out for you?"

Beau had no answer.

You said there was a second reason." Bryce asked. "What is it?"

"The door to the shed's around side of the building. Hiding behind it is fine, but if you want a peek inside, you're gonna have to go around. You'll be out in the open, right in Myers' sights."

Bryce didn't want to tell them he was afraid she might have tampered with the tank. Instead he moved on. "Since we've exhausted our options with regard to getting away, it's time to think of a way to get help to come up here. Lyn's plan to try the cell phones is a good start." He turned to her. "You should head outside now and see what you can get. If anyone's got a phone they haven't given her, hand it over now." Bryce waited while everyone kept sitting on their hands. "Okay. Now, assuming she's right and there's no signal here worth a squirt of piss, the next best option is that I get to my car so I can radio back to base. I'm parked..." He hesitated a moment, unsure how he was going to explain the next part. "I'm parked across the highway in Ms. Myer's driveway. We're going to have to come up with some kind of diversion so I can get over there without getting shot." He neglected to add the word, "Again."

"No fuckin' way," Luis shouted. "I already seen what 'a diversion' means to you people, and I ain't getting my head blown off so you can make a phone call."

"It's not just a phone call. It's—"

"Don't bother trying to reason with him," Hunter interrupted. He wouldn't have the balls to do it anyway." Lyn squeezed his hands tighter and shushed him softly and the boy's tense shoulders eased a little.

"Does that mean you're going to go running out there?"

"No one is running out there," Neil said weakly. He was looking bad and seemed to be fading in and out of consciousness, but he demonstrated that he'd been listening. "We have to think of some other way. Joanie's already shown that she's willing to take a shot at any one of us."

"What about Leonard?" Luis asked.

"What about him? Chickenshit ran away as soon as the windows broke," Beau said. "Did *you* see a big Indian cook outside, officer? Alive or dead?"

"I didn't."

"Well, he got away then. I say we take our chances with the rock slide."

"We can't carry Neil and Carol down the scree slope," Lyn said. "We'll *all* break our necks."

"And how is that my problem?" Luis asked.

"That's enough," Bryce interrupted. "I've had enough of your attitude." *The kid was pinging my Spidey-sense before he started talking. Now that he's opened his mouth I'm pretty sure if I go through his pockets I'll come up with a half dozen reasons why I wouldn't trust him with my drink order, let alone our lives.* "Lyn, can you go outside and make some calls? Beau and me are going to take a peek at that shed. *From* cover, don't worry. The rest of you can stay put and wait for us to return. If you hear anybody come through in the front, I want you out the back right away, got it?" Everyone nodded their heads in agreement.

Before heading for the door, Beau ducked into his office. He emerged holding the hunting rifle from the wall above his desk. Lyn yelped and scrambled toward the far wall, fumbling in her apron for her gun.

Bryce stepped in between Lyn and her manager, blocking their aim at each other. "What are you doing?" he asked Beau, his hand hovering over his sidearm. "Do I need to be more worried about what's going on between the two of you than what's happening out front?"

"We're good. I'll show you the shed," Beau said, hefting the rifle up in front of him. "But, from here on out, I ain't going anywhere without protection." He looked over Bryce's shoulder at Lyn. "You understand. We're on the same team, right?"

She nodded. Bryce wasn't sure if it was progress, but he'd take it.

1640 hrs

Bryce followed Beau around the side of the building trying to stay as flat against the wall as he could. "That's it," Beau said, nodding his head to a structure growing off of the side of the restaurant like a slatted pine tumor ten feet in front of them. "Doors are on the side facing the trees. See? It's suicide."

"You said they're locked."

"Yep. It's got a heavy duty swinging latch and a padlock on the front."

"Give me your keys," Bryce demanded.

Beau looked at him with a badly-acted look of confusion on his face. "What for? I told you: only two keys I know of open that lock, and neither of 'em is here."

"Just because I'm not going to make you look like a liar in front of everyone else doesn't mean I believe you," he said, spitting tobacco juice onto the gravel between them. He wiped a dribble off his chin with the back of his hand and absently smeared it on the seat of his brown uniform pants. "It'd be irresponsible not to keep a copy of the key here in case something went wrong. What if the gas line came loose? You want me to buy that you're going to let propane leak out for an hour or more while you wait for Idaho P and G to come up here with a c-clamp? It's either in your desk or on your keyring. And I'm betting that a guy like you likes to have all of his keys with him all the time." He nodded down at the lumpy bulge in the front of Beau's too-tight Wrangler jeans. "I know you're not that happy to see me."

Beau fished in his front pocket and pulled out a ring of keys.

"What's your angle here?" Bryce asked.

"I think you're suicidal. We don't need to draw her attention to the shed. You walk around and unlock that door and here come the armor piercing flying straight as angry yellow jackets. I don't feel like getting blown up today. How 'bout you?" He asked through gritted teeth, grinding hard on his soggy, flattened toothpick.

"You might not have a choice about that if she's decided this is her backup plan."

"I'm not waiting around here for you to draw her fire." He turned to leave.

Bryce grabbed Beau's arm hard. "You're going to stand there and answer my damn questions when I ask them. If you tell any more little lies, like *'there are only two keys,'* Joanie is going to be the least of your worries. You copy that?" Beau nodded and stood pouting against the wall with his arms folded, rifle slung over his shoulder like a kid who got told he's not good enough to take the shot. *Jesus, he's less mature than my son.* Bryce wondered how a man like this could be trusted to run a restaurant, and then answered his own question. *It's not a restaurant. He's running a trick bag. Keep the place lit up and active until Joanie breaks and agrees to sell her home to the man who always gets what he wants. If anybody asks, it isn't extortion or harassment–
–just a business venture. Well, you got what you wanted. She broke all right.*

Bryce sidled up to the edge of the shed. The structure was big enough for a fifteen-hundred gallon bulk tank and a generator. Joanie's place had a similar set up. That one was only five-hundred gallons, however, and didn't have to be filled as often. It was also set farther away from the house, for what Bryce assumed were safety reasons. At the top of the shed ran a six-inch tall wire mesh window for ventilation, which extended along the edge below the roof. He tried to peek in through the mesh, but could only see the tank. Nothing below it was in view. *Inside, I need to see inside.* He peeked around the corner of the shed and spied the latch and lock that Beau described. He said a short prayer and slipped around the corner, leaving the manager standing alone below the access ladder leading to the roof.

1640 hrs

Lyn flipped open her phone and looked for the little bar icon to light up, even though she knew it wouldn't have a signal. *Shitty free phone barely gets a single bar in town.* It was yet another reason she wanted to leave for greener pastures. The screen on the out-of-date, out-of-style clamshell read: *SEARCHING FOR SIGNAL.* She stuffed her cell in the right pocket of her apron and pulled Beau's *iPhone* out of the left. He used it constantly, keeping track of the employees' shift schedule and the register till on the device. But she never saw him talking on it; he used the landline to make calls. The signal icon was the same. *No Signal.* Next. The *Blackberry* belonged to Neil. She wasn't sure how to use it with its big keyboard, but did her best. When she finally woke it up she could see that he had several unread messages but no signal, like all the rest. *SEARCHING. Fuck!* As she was slipping the device into her "used" pocket it vibrated in her hand. Pulling it back out she looked again at the screen. "Holy shit! A bar." She squeaked a little and almost jumped in excitement. She pinched the card Bryce had given her with the Idaho State Police number on it tightly and dialed. It rang a few times before a woman answered. She sounded like she was talking through a potato chip bag.

"I don't know how long I have to say this," Lyn spat. She struggled to remember all of the information that Bryce told her to give the State Patrol. "We're being held hostage at *Your Mountain Home Kitchen* on Route 1A. Deputy Bryce Douglas of the Boundary County Sheriff's department says you need to set up road blocks and shut down traffic on the road before sending help."

"Slow down-*CRACKLE*-Who is this?" asked the distant voice.

"Just listen, and do what I say. A whole bunch of people are dead and some are shot. We need the police and an ambulance up here now."

"Can't underst-*CRACKLE*-your location-*CRACKLE*-speak slowly."

"Damn it! We're at *Your* fucking *Mountain Home Kitchen* on Route 1A! Send cops. Send paramedics. Send help! She's still got us pinned down and we can't get out."

"*CRACKLE*-say again? *CRACKLE*-situation?"

"Joanie Myer. Joanie Myer is killing us all. She shot a cop and she'll kill everyone unless you come help us." Lyn looked at the screen that read,

SIGNAL LOST. She fought the urge to dash it against the side of the building. Instead, she redialed and got the same woman's distorted voice before the call dropped again. Staring at the phone in frustration, she watched as the text message counter changed from a four to five.

The signal's only strong enough for texts. But, I can't text a landline.

Lyn keyed in her mom's cell number and composed a message. *It's Lyn. No signal up here. Borrowing friends phone. Call cops!!! Shooting @ YMHK need ambulance need COPS!!! No joke! CALL THEM NOW!!!* She stabbed the send button and watched with anticipation as the outgoing message icon went from red to green. *MESSAGE DELIVERED.* The list of people she knew who would even open a text from an unfamiliar number instead of assuming it was spam and deleting it was frustratingly small. *Now, if Mom isn't too tipsy to read it.*

She sighed and leaned against the wall, feeling something close to relief for the first time since the shooting started. She slid down and sat in the gravel, staring off into the forest below. Lyn loved to take her break behind the restaurant. Sometimes she'd smoke a little and stare into the lush valley as she felt the peace of the Selkirk Mountains shrink her down to size. She could sit and just be a part of something larger than the hostess station or the dining room. The beauty of the verdant forest always helped her place the frustrations of the day in context. No demanding customer, sore back, or belligerent manager could compete with the fertile green mountain view spreading out for miles, unspoiled by roads or swaths cut for ski lifts and trails.

She looked into the woods and remembered the last time her grandfather had taken her camping when she was only fourteen. After two days of sleeping in tents, swimming, fishing, and hiking, they relaxed under the stars to take in their last night together before heading home in the morning. "You know, kiddo, you've had to grow up way too fast," he'd said. "What with your daddy leavin' and your mom, well... bein' the way she is." He paused to contemplate how his own daughter was coping with the demise of her marriage. Lyn knew her Grampa was afraid that any day now she'd become more interested in shopping and boys and whatever else it was that young women liked to do instead of spending the weekend in the forest sawing firewood and tying fishing lures with old men. Lyn knew that she'd never get tired of their trips, but he'd already lived through that same rejection with his daughter and—like a virus—the fear was in him; he was going to lose her, too. So, one night, he just started talking while they lay on a plastic tarp spread out near—but not too near—the fire, staring up at the stars through the forest canopy. She listened to his voice reverberate in his chest. His sweet breath permanently scented with pipe tobacco softly caressed her hair while he spoke.

"Mentally, I was where you are now when then sent me off to Vietnam. Growin' up but not a grown-up. When you get saddled with all sorts of sudden responsibility they never tell you how to shoulder the weight; they just expect you to do it.

"I used to lie on my back in that jungle, scared shitless, and look at the stars and think about how small the planet is," he said. "I used to lie there and look up and think about how the Earth was this tiny little speck o'dust floatin' around with all the billions and billions of other stuff in space. And the smaller the planet got, the closer I was to your Grandma and your mom, who was just a little baby then. Thinkin' about it that way, it didn't seem so hard to get back to what mattered—to the people I love. And *all* that mattered in 'Nam was getting home to those people. The smaller everything got, the less different the jungle was from the place we are now and I was just this little part of it, lyin' in the night, lookin' at the same stars your grandma could see. I was thinkin' 'bout how at the end of the day, no matter how bad things got, everything that meant something to me was just on the other side of this tiny... little... thing. Barely a footstep or two away if you think about it like that. Everything worthwhile in my life was right there with me. Keepin' me centered. Keepin' me safe."

She hadn't asked him to tell her how he coped with fear during the war, but he'd sensed that she was dealing with something bigger than herself since her dad had run off. He knew she needed a pep-talk, and whether he was really talking about Vietnam or the cancer he never told anyone he had, he knew that she had an empty spot inside of her that needed to be filled with something that would make her strong. Something she could lean against when she was sure she couldn't stand up on her own any longer.

"Why are you telling me this, Grampa?" she said, not wanting him to stop talking. Not wanting the deep rumble of his voice in his chest to go silent.

"So if you ever feel like things are getting' to be too much and closin' in on you, you know to think about the forest and the mountains and the sky and the stars—all those things that are bigger'n you, they're tiny, too. And wherever you want to be, wherever it is that's *safe*, well, that's just a little bit away on this little tiny thing we're livin' on. You *can* get there. Do you understand what I'm sayin'?"

Staring out at the valley below *Your Mountain Home Kitchen*, Lyn whispered, "I do. I get it now." An enveloping feeling of being small and cradled in the middle of something majestic centered her—gave her hope. Escape wasn't that far away.

Scattered about the mountainsides were patches of yellow and purple wildflowers. Small blue ponds glinted in the light reflecting the wide, tranquil sky. *It's so beautiful,* she thought. The distant shining mountains standing above the valley shade helped her forget the pain in her cut up hands and legs. And then the countryside told her what she should've already known. *This is why Joanie bought her place. She used to look out her window and see* this *before Adam and Beau set up shop.*

She thought of all the things that *she'd* lost over time: her father, her grandfather, her mother's attention, her brother's companionship and confidence. None of those things had been ripped away. They'd slipped out of her life, one at a time, slowly, like erosion wearing down a hillside, forcing her to become someone new. She could cope with gradual change; it had made her who she was—the person who keeps the job she hates, pays the rent, fixes meals and helps her mother to bed at night because she has to— and because she's strong enough. But in the middle of everything that was expected of her, she had this retreat—this oasis of tranquility—to help her shoulder the weight of responsibility.

And Lyn understood.

This is what she *needed to keep her life together. Joanie counted on this to make her whole. And they ruined it.*

Pulling Beau's *iPhone* out of her pocket, she poked at his *contacts* button and scrolled down, stopping at *Bischoff, Adam S.* She pulled up his cell number. *Are you sure you want to do this?* She thought about the people lying dead in the dining room—about the doctor bleeding to death and the kid who might lose his father and the woman who already lost everything she loved. *It's your fault. It's your fault all these people are dead and I'm going to die and never see my mom or brother again. I'm never going to move to New York and become a designer because* you *want to buy someone else's house. Well, fuck you.*

She started typing out a text message. *J.Myer in YMHK. Says READY TO SELL. U need 2 come up NOW!* Her finger hovered over the SEND icon.

Out of the corner of her eye, she thought she saw something moving in the woods. Something that crept in the darkness on the edges of her perception, between dream and reality. Something giant and black with a wolf's face and antlers. She tried not to look. *You are not going crazy, Lynnea. You are not seeing that. Please don't lose it, girl.* Staring at the phone, she watched the signal bar. A cloud moved away from the sun, bathing her in light, and the last little tiny rectangle on the left of the screen turned white.

She hit SEND and closed her eyes.

The something in the woods beside her huffed.

1643 hrs

The phone vibrated on the table in the corner and a short burst of a twangy song extolling the listener to call someone who cares made the figure beside it grunt and shift in his chair. He stared wide-eyed at the device, so close, but out of reach. Joanie rolled over onto an elbow and looked across the room at him. "Who do you think that is?" she asked.

He had no answer. Though he could breathe through the hole in the ball, its jaw-spreading girth prevented him from making anything more than stupid animal sounds. That seemed fitting, since he'd made the gag out of a Kong dog ball and leather collar she'd bought online. "Great for tough chewers," the packaging had read. She thought at first that she'd overestimated the size of the ball, but then, he had a big mouth. Even though it looked painful, and his jaw popped when she jammed it in, it fit.

He breathed harshly through the hole in the center of it—his broken nose offering no clear passage of air. Saliva sputtered out when he exhaled, dripping onto his lap. A long, gossamer string of spittle dangled from his chin and sparkled in the afternoon light like a thread of spider's silk.

Joanie pushed up off her platform and crossed the room. She reached for the phone on the table and he flinched. She smiled and swiped across the screen with the finger she'd used to kill several people. There was no passcode to unlock the phone. No one touched his things. Who would ever dare intrude upon his privacy?

She read the text and couldn't suppress a gasp. His eyebrows turned up in confusion and then fear as her mouth curved up into a cruel grin. She took a step forward and held the phone in front of him so he could see. He flinched away from her again, but eventually turned his face toward the screen.

"Your friend wants you to come join the party, Adam. I thought Beau was your boy. How does that make you feel?" She looked again at the text and let out a single breathy laugh. "Yeah. I'd be upset too. I suppose now you want me to get back to work." He shook his head, breathing quickly through the ball. She almost wanted to take it out and ask him again, but given the things he'd been prone to say to her in the past when he was able, she knew she had no interest in his insights or observations. All she wanted from him was a witness. She wanted him to see with open eyes what he'd set in motion.

She put the phone down on the table and set herself back to work. She'd turned away too long already. She didn't want to miss a thing.

1643 hrs

Beau checked his watch again for the fourth time, though it had only been a couple of minutes since the cop had slipped around the wall. He'd been waiting for the sound of the shot to echo through the valley. Listening for the signal to go back inside the restaurant and... do what? Lyn had lost it and had a gun to back herself up. *But I have a gun, too.* He adjusted the strap of the rifle on his shoulder again, feeling a small sense of confidence in its power. Military or not, Beau wasn't about to be bullied by someone who'd probably sat back at the base fixing meals or fixing trucks while real soldiers faced the enemy. And he sure as hell wasn't about to be outdone in a crisis by a waitress either.

I'd feel a hell of a lot better if she didn't have that damned Glock. What do I do? I can't just go ask for it. Reason with her to give it to someone with more sense. Who is that anyway? The kid from town? The doctor? No. She isn't going to give it up without a fight.

Rubbing his hand over his face, he banished the thought from his mind. He'd said they were working together. He'd have to let her have it for the time being and hope that the policeman kept jumping in between them whenever she felt froggy—*if* he lived through his adventure in the shed. Until then, he just had to wait.

And then it occurred to him. A movie he'd seen about a pair of snipers stalking each other through Leningrad or Stalingrad or some Othergrad during World War II crept into his mind. Ed Harris was in it. He couldn't remember if he'd played the Nazi or the Commie, but it didn't matter. What did make a difference was that there was a way out of this. There was a way for him to take care of everything and hand it to Adam like a big present wrapped up in a bow. She was giving him the opportunity to show the boss what he was capable of.

Thank you, Joanie.

He looked at the steel ladder. Like all roofs in northern Idaho, the restaurant's was pitched—but not too steeply. He could climb up, lean over the ridge, and take his time lining up a shot. He'd have cover behind the field of the roof for everything but his head. *She ain't expecting anyone to climb up there and fight back. If I keep low, she'll never see me.*

Jumping up, he caught the bottom rung and hauled himself up, scrambling over the fascia as quickly as he could to get out of sight. Normally, getting up on the roof, he took his time, being careful to have a steady footing. Unlike in the winter, however, when he had to climb up to shove off accumulated snow, it wasn't too slippery. It was a steep enough pitch that he had to be careful, but not too bad.

On top, he lay back for a few seconds catching his breath. Leaning to the side, he slung the rifle off his back and rolled over onto his stomach. Doing the military crawl up to the ridge was harder than he anticipated in cowboy boots. Gravity and the angled surface conspired to pull him back to earth, but he kept his focus trained on the task and reached the top without sliding down and off into space. He held on to the ridge and peeked over.

Hoping to have as direct a view into Joanie's house as he could manage, he'd crept at an angle toward the middle of the building. From there, however, the restaurant sign blocked much of his view of her house, so he shuffled closer to the edge to see around it. He silently thanked whoever had clear-cut the trees from the front of her property. It was likely so whoever had built the house originally could have a good view of the valley behind him. It had also meant that she couldn't pretend, from behind the full leaves, that *Your Mountain Home Kitchen* didn't exist. And now it meant that he had a clear line of sight right into the house.

The main picture window in the front was broken. He could see her dog sleeping next to the breakfast table, but nothing else. He brought the rifle around over the ridge and looked through the scope. The animal wasn't sleeping. His stomach turned at the sight of the dog and he thought about his two black labs at home, waiting, wondering when he was going to let them out of their run to streak around the yard. Who was going to throw the ball and open the cans of food and scratch their bellies? If it was possible for Beau to think less of Joanie, he did now. He promised himself that when he got the shot, he'd treat himself to three of the biggest steaks from the freezer tonight. One for him, and the others for Slim and Coe.

He tracked along the front of the house, searching, and saw nothing. The first floor windows were empty and the curtains were pulled upstairs. *Where the holy hell is she?* The feeling of assurance and authority of the rifle in his hands was waning. He was beginning to feel nervous again, having had his head in sight too long. He stole a glance at his watch. Four forty-seven. Time was stretching out and moving slowly. *I've got time. Take it.*

Thinking about what Luis had said about his cousin the Marine sniper, he took a deep breath and tried to remain patient. He wasn't going to wait three days or piss in his Wranglers, but he wasn't about to start popping off rounds either in the hope that he *might* hit something and draw Joanie's attention right to him. *That's not how it's done. Get the target in the crosshairs. Stay calm. One clean shot.*

He imagined taking the shot. He thought about returning a triumphant hero and announcing to everyone that he'd done what he'd had to. *I take no pleasure in killing, but a man does...*

The crack sounded a half second after the shingles in front of him exploded, pelting his face and arms with rough fiberglass and asphalt debris. His hand jerked in fear and the rifle discharged. The kick of the gun shook it from his hands and the thing went sliding down the front of the restaurant as he lost his own purchase and slid down the opposite side. Digging in with his boots and fingernails he worked to slow his descent before he slid right off the end and into the back lot. A few of his nails bent backward painfully and the searing pain in his index finger suggested that that one tore clean off.

"Oh Jesus, Lord, not like this! *Notlikethis!*"

He felt his toes go over the edge and his shins bang against the gutter. He wrenched his back to the side and flung an arm out for the slender pipe vent stack. Pain lanced through his shoulder and neck as the weight of his body pulled and wrenched the awkwardly twisted arm. But he held on. And he stopped sliding.

Beau lay his face against the hot, rough shingles and breathed heavily. His heart beat in his chest against the roof and thrummed deafeningly in his ears. He felt almost certain they'd be able to hear his panic and fear inside the restaurant like the drum beat from one of those super woofer setups that rattled the windows when kids drove by in their cars.

He breathed.

And he held on.

He thought about climbing up to see what had happened to his rifle. It was lost, though. *Even if it got hung up in the rain gutter, I can't go scrambling down to get it. She'll see me.*

She saw me.

And she stopped me. He realized she'd done it without killing him, too. Maybe she'd missed because he was behind cover and she just wasn't as good as she thought she was. Or maybe, she was saving him for last. Just like Lyn suggested. Making his end drag out.

Beau took another breath and started inching for the ladder. If he was going to die, he'd do it on his feet, and not hanging half off the roof like the guy who can't take the shot.

This failure stung worse than anything he'd ever felt in his life.

1643 hrs

Bryce flattened himself against the wall of the shed. His instinct was to crouch, but that meant facing away from the wall and toward Joanie. He forced himself to present a slimmer profile target. *No matter what direction I face, there's no making my head any smaller.*

He reached the door. From a distance it looked fine, but up close he saw the padlock hanging off the lock arm, which was swung over to look closed, but wasn't latched. He nudged the door open a little wider with his wounded arm and slipped inside, pulling it closed behind him quickly.

Inside, it was stifling hot and, despite the vent grate, the place stank of exhaust from the generator. The propane tank was enormous and nearly filled the entire space. At the far end, enclosed in a metal case, the generator rumbled and growled. He pulled the six-battery MagLite from his gun belt and clicked it on before moving to the generator hatch to get a look at the control panel. The only controls were an on/off switch, an emergency cut off, and a reset button. *If we're here after sundown, do we want the lights?* He didn't know; he'd never been in a siege before.

Bryce hit the emergency cut off. The device wasn't high tech enough to send a signal to the company, but at least the darkened restaurant might discourage other potential customers from stopping. As the motor wound down and his ears adjusted to the growing silence he felt a pang of despair creep into his guts. *Dark and quiet. That was what we need to slip away. Except, that's what she needs to slip in as well. I bet that damned rifle of hers has a night scope. Shit, Logan's got* toy *goggles with night vision.*

The tank was flush up against the wall. He peeked behind it as best he could with the flashlight but didn't see anything out of the ordinary. Not satisfied, but not convinced that she'd tampered with it either, he toyed with the idea of waiting Joanie out right there.

"Come on, Deputy," he said. "People are counting on you." He stepped from behind the control box and walked right into Leonard Blackbear and his big, glinting Bowie knife.

Bryce jumped at the sound of gunfire outside. The big man didn't flinch.

1650 hrs

Lyn guiltily tried to stuff Beau's *iPhone* in her pocket as he crept around the building. "You done with that?" he asked, holding out his hand.

"What the hell happened over there? Who was shooting? Is Bryce all right? Did you give him your rifle?"

"Give me my phone." He stood holding out a badly scratched palm. Blood and something black caked his fingernails. She fished the overpriced toy out of her apron and handed it over.

"I couldn't get through to anybody." She kept glancing at the trees, looking for Bryce—or the thing haunting the shadows—but saw nothing. "We're on our own."

Beau nodded but he didn't say, I told you so. She could see his jaw flexing, working overtime, grinding away at what was left of his pick. She never saw the remains of one. She wondered if he swallowed them. She tried to figure out what the look on his face meant. She wasn't sure if it was fear or sadness or just resignation. Was he seeing things creeping in the shadows, too? Whatever it was, it wasn't a look she'd ever seen him wear before. He looked defeated.

If he's trying to get sympathy he's out of luck. What was it grampa used to say about sympathy? You can find it between shit and syphilis in the dictionary. She pushed herself up from the ground and brushed the dust off the rear of her skirt. "Where's Bryce?" she asked.

"Back there," he said, jerking his thumb over his shoulder.

"You ass! You left him? Is that what the shooting was? Is he okay?"

"Sorry if I didn't want to hang around to see him get aerated." Beau's slumped shoulders pulled back as he stood up straight. "And another thing, I'm tired of you and your shit. Whether we get out of this or not, you're fired."

She stuck a finger in his chest and replied, "Whether or not we get out of this, you're a cunt."

Beau slapped Lyn hard across the face, knocking her down. A couple of cell phones, her sketchbook and the Glock fell out of her pocket. He kicked the book away toward the edge of the lot and reached down to pluck the handgun out of the gravel. "That's enough out of that mouth. I can see why you'd be friends with the psycho across the highway." Lyn got on her knees and looked up at her boss. He crouched down in front of her and asked, "Think you ought to say 'sorry?'" She spit a mouthful of blood in his face. He punched her with a closed fist knocking her flat on her back. Lyn stayed on the gravel this time, rolling over, unwilling to let him see her cry. She felt her numbing upper lip and her fingers came away bloody. Her bottom lip was definitely split and her nose felt broken. Between her own blood, and the bad tippers' blood and brains, she felt like she'd never be clean again.

"You made me do that," Beau said. He was panting. "And now, without this, you can forget about acting all high an—" Lyn threw two handfuls of gravel in his face and interrupted his threat. He lurched back, sputtering on the dirt and pebbles in his mouth. She jumped up and followed him, rearing back and swinging the hardest kick she'd thrown since seventh grade soccer. It hurt her foot to kick him as hard as she did—she thought she might even have broken a toe on his pelvis—but she got the sense it hurt his balls more. And that's what she wanted. He gagged and clutched at his aching balls before falling where he'd knocked her a second earlier. The gun fell out of his hands into the gravel.

She picked it up and kicked him a second and third time in the stomach for good measure before spitting on him again. A red mess of blood and saliva splatted in his face and she wished she work up another expectoration, but her mouth had gone dry. She dashed over to where her Moleskine had come to rest next to the dumpster. Dusting off the cover, she replaced the elastic band across the front and embraced it tightly for as long as she could bear to hold her breath. Finally, she walked calmly back over to where Beau lay, gasping for air.

"If you touch me again I'll kill you. I'll shoot you in the fucking guts and make you drag your sorry ass out the front door to ask Joanie for help, you pig." She turned on her heel and stormed into the restaurant.

Inside, Hunter and Luis were engaged in a staring contest. "What happened to you?" Hunter asked. Raylynne gasped and Luis laughed at Lyn's visibly broken nose. Letting the door close behind her with a bang and a click, she stuffed the sketchbook in her pocket, strode over to her locker, and grabbed her backpack. Slinging it over her shoulder she slammed the metal door with a loud clang and turned toward Luis who was still laughing. She aimed the gun at him and said, "See something funny, pussy?" His amusement died abruptly. The feeling she had inside that something had changed in her was becoming as clear to everyone else as the swelling nose on her face.

"You going somewhere, *bonita*?" he asked.

"I'm going to the ladies' room to wash my face and change my clothes. When I get back, if you've moved from that spot, I'll shoot you."

"What if one of us has to pee?" Raylynne asked.

"Just him. The rest of you do whatever you want."

"That's not fair—"

"Fair? What's that?" she asked, holding up his gun for him to see. "This is mine. I took it. Do you think there's anything else of yours I can't take as long as I have this?" Leaning in, she said, "Look in my face. Fair has left for the day. Do you think it's coming back?"

"No."

"Fuckin' A." Lyn stepped away from Luis, feeling a moment's hesitation at turning her back even though she was mostly certain that the sweet smell drifting up at her was fresh urine staining his pants. She walked briskly around the corner. Everyone watched her in the mirror as she pushed defiantly through the swinging doors leading into the dining room like she had just been promoted to assistant manager.

1650 hrs

Bryce struggled to remain calm despite the distinct rifle reports outside: Joanie's sniper weapon and the more familiar sound of a thirty-aught hunting rifle. Beau's gun. He tried not to imagine the worst. He listened, waiting for more sounds while keeping his eyes on the man standing in front of him. No screaming, no more shots. A minute later, he heard a deep thump and crunch, like someone jumping down from something and walking away. *What in God's name are you doing, Beau?* He tried to contain his anxiety and focus on the present situation.

"You must be Leonard."

"What does it matter who I am?"

"Look, I'm not here to start anything." Bryce nodded at the knife in the big man's hand. "I don't care why a cook in a roadside diner brings a Bowie knife with him to work. All I want is to make sure that this tank isn't wired to blow."

Leonard's eyes narrowed. "What do you mean, 'wired to blow'?"

"I mean," the woman who's been shooting the place up is military trained and combat tested. If she didn't just snap this morning, then she's got a contingency plan to take care of people who try to run out the back. Or hide in the shed. My guess is, when she gets bored of waiting for us to pop up into her crosshairs, she presses the Plan B button and this tank will go up in a big ball of fire taking the restaurant and everything inside with it."

"Woman?"

"Yeah. Joanie Myer from across the way. The one you're all up here to torture. She's a combat-trained sniper. But I don't know if she's also qualified in demolitions, so 'Plan B' might go off by accident if your cell phone is on the same frequency as her transmitter. If it's all the same to you, I'd prefer you put down the knife and help me take a look."

Leonard's hand wavered. "How do I know you're not messing with me?"

"While you've been in here, have you noticed any little red lights that don't belong on a propane tank? Since I shut down the generator have you heard anything like a beep?"

"I can't hear shit with you buzzing in my ear. Shut up a minute." Leonard cocked his head to listen, pushing back a black braid away to cup a hand behind his ear. Despite his size, if he'd had two good arms, Bryce figured he could have the man disarmed and on the ground after only a bit of a struggle. With a shattered shoulder and an arm in a sling he knew all he would get out of making any sudden moves was split open like a trophy buck. "I don't hear anything," Leonard said.

"You mind letting me take a look? Or are we going to keep standing here like this?"

Leonard hesitated, then nodded. But he didn't lower the knife. "Go 'head."

Bryce squatted down and saw exactly what he feared most. Although he knew little about explosives, he figured what was stuck to the bottom of the tank was enough to ignite its contents. And he knew enough that on a Sunday, there was still enough in the freshly filled tank to take out most of the restaurant, starting with the employee area on the opposite side of the wall where everyone was huddled. "Take a look at this," he said, waving the big man down to his level. Leonard squatted and hissed through his teeth. "No shit," Bryce agreed.

A black plastic toolbox was stuck underneath the tank, almost invisible in the shadows. He moved his flashlight to get a look at different angles. Under any other circumstances, Bryce would have thought it just a convenient place to store the tools necessary to service or fine-tune the lines feeding fuel into the restaurant. He'd have rationalized the shape away as something else, even though he knew there was no good reason for a toolbox to have a radio receiver glued to the end of it, or there for to be wires connecting them. Any fool could see it was a detonator. He wanted to slide the box out, open it, and look at whatever Joanie had left for them. He had no idea how she'd fail-safed the device, however. Opening it seemed like a short road to detonating the contents, which, he could only imagine, were powerful enough to end his days if they could ignite the tank.

"What do we do? Can you disarm it?" Leonard asked.

"Damned if I know how. Do you see a switch?"

"It can't be that easy. Can it?"

"I doubt it. My guess is, if this is Joanie's backup plan, then there's probably also a redun... another backup built into the detonator." He wiped away the sweat dripping in his eyes and spat. Leonard flinched with the knife and Bryce nearly let go of his bowels. "Jesus! You mind putting that thing away already? You've got bigger problems than me." Leonard looked at the blade, considering it for a moment before stuffing it into the sheath in the back of his checkered chef's trousers. "Thanks," Bryce said.

"You bet. So, how do we turn it off without triggering her redundancy measure?"

Bryce blinked rapidly, trying to put in context what he'd just heard coming from the machete-wielding American Indian cook who was rumored to be selling dope out of his diner. "We don't," he finally said. He hadn't ever seen a bomb before, but he'd been sent to counter-terrorist training in Portland when Sheriff Winter needed to spend Department of Homeland Security money so he could guarantee more next year, and maybe a big armored vehicle to play in too. That's where Bryce had learned that if an explosive device went off, he still needed to call the bomb squad (he thought the State

Patrol might have someone who could do that job). Al Qaeda learned from the IRA that a bomb drew first responders, who you could then kill with a secondary explosive. Joanie wasn't Al Qaeda, and this wasn't Belfast, but Bryce wasn't willing to bet that she didn't have a backup device on the other side of the tank or at least a trigger that set this one off if someone tried to shut it down.

"You can stay here if you want," he told Leonard. "You're out of sight as long as you keep your head low, or—"

"My ass! There's a bomb in here."

"Or, I was about to say, you can follow me inside and we'll come up with our own Plan B." Bryce knocked his knuckles against the propane tank making Leonard nearly leap out the shed door.

"Don't fuckin' do that, man."

"Yeah, *that* probably wasn't a good idea. Neither is this: I want you to slip out that door as quickly as you can, keeping your back to the wall until you can get around the corner to cover. I'll be right behind you."

"No way, white man. I'll be right behind *you*."

Bryce and Leonard studied each other uncertainly for a moment, but neither moved. With his hand on the butt of his gun, Bryce said, "Look, I want you to know that today I have no interest in what goes on day to day in this place, or why you come to work armed. All I want to know is whether it's a bad idea for me to let you have my back." Leonard shook his head. Bryce couldn't tell whether he was saying it was or wasn't a bad idea. The big man's face was as unreadable as a sphinx. "I'm going to trust that you're on my side today. Is that a trust we share?"

Leonard nodded.

"Okay then. Let's get out of here and see what fresh hell is going on outside."

Leonard's brow furrowed. "Still, why don't *you* go first?"

"Because by the time she's seen you and taken aim I'll be stepping out the door in between you and her shot. That is, unless you want to leave second and be the target. I'll gladly take the head start."

"When you put it that way..." Leonard moved for the door. Before he could push it open, Bryce laid a hand on his shoulder.

"Slip out. Don't fling the door. We're both better off if she doesn't see us at all. Got it?" This was Leonard's big test. *If he can be trusted to follow this direction, then maybe he'll be a good ally to have inside the restaurant when it's time to get everyone out.* The cook nodded. "All right. Let's go."

An explosion outside rocked the little shed. Bryce clenched up waiting for the bigger bang to engulf them both.

I'm sorry, Cherie. I tried.

Leonard grabbed him roughly by the shirt and hauled him out the door. "No time to pray!"

1653 hrs

Luis looked at the people trapped in the employees' room with him. Everyone was staring his way. Everyone knew Lyn had made him piss in his pants. He pushed himself up from the floor and dusted off like he could brush away urine. Like he could brush away the shame he felt for having been put in his place by both a woman and a fourteen-year-old boy.

"What do you think you're doing?" Hunter asked. He'd coiled up ready to dive for Luis's center of gravity as soon as he reached his feet. "Lyn said not to move."

"Think I give a shit what she said? I ain't waiting for her to get back and shoot me because she thinks I scratched my ass. Fuck all y'all." Luis made a grand gesture, waving at the others with fingers extended like cocked guns, and started to stalk off toward the door.

"Where do you think you're going to go?" Raylynne asked. "Whatshername's out there waiting to shoot us, too."

"I'm taking my chances down the hill. Even if I break my fuckin' leg, it's still better'n gettin' shot by either one of these crazy bitches. If you're smart you'll come with me." Luis walked up to Hunter, leaned over, and jerked back his hand like he was going to punch the boy. Hunter didn't flinch. He waited. "Faggot. I hope your old man bleeds to death." With his middle finger up, he walked to the back door and kicked it open. It thumped against something outside and slammed shut. Luis leaned in and shoved it open roughly before peeking out to see what he'd hit.

Beau lay unconscious in the gravel, blood trickling from his forehead.

"I quit, *puta*," he told the manager and walked off, letting the door slam behind him.

Outside in the sun, it felt like nothing was wrong. There was no crazed sniper waiting to blow his brains out. There was no crazed waitress threatening to blow his brains out. There was nothing but him and daylight and freedom. Almost as if he could walk out front, get in his car, and drive home for some endo and a beer. He walked past the dumpsters to the edge of the lot and peered down the sheer rock slide leading to the trees below. *I can do this. Go down on my ass and go slow. Ain't nothin' but nothin'.*

He sat, dangling his legs over the edge. A few rocks trickled down the slope. He waited for them to kick up larger boulders and start an avalanche like he'd seen in cartoons. When they didn't, he knew he was on his way home. *Fuckin' idiots.*

The first few feet were slippery, but he eventually got the hang of it. He half crab walked, half slid on his butt over the rocks that had been blown out of the mountain to make the road and lot above. As he approached the tree line, he felt less ashamed for having pissed himself. *I made it. I made it down the hill and I'm going to make it out of here. And when they report this shit on the news, I'll be all like—*

He didn't see the thin wire extending across the space in between two boulders on either side of him. He heard a faint pinging and a tinkle of metal, then felt a second's heat from the grenades that scorched and blasted him and dashed his splintered remains against the rocks before sending them raining down into the evergreens below.

1657 hrs

Dressing in her own clothes gave Lyn the feeling that she'd finally regained a semblance of control over her life—even if it was an illusion. In reality, she was still trapped in a diner. Changing her clothes in the bathroom gave her the same amount of control over her life as a condemned prisoner ordering his last meal. It wouldn't make any difference how she looked when the bullet that took her life finally found her.

She looked at the green peasant frock that hung loosely over skinny jeans emphasizing a little too well how skinny she really was. She pulled on her boots and finally buckled the wide belt around her waist. *This is who I am.* Carefully sliding the gun into her belt, she looked into the mirror and said, "This is who I've become."

Washing her face wasn't as painful as seeing what Beau had done to her once narrow, straight nose. She scrubbed at the skin under her eyes until she realized that they were black from bruising, not filth. She parted her fingers and looked at the gun in her belt, wondering whether she'd feel a bullet rip through her skull before her brains gave out and she could just go to sleep. She doubted there would be any difference if the bullet came from Joanie's gun or her own. Leaning against the sink, trying to banish the thought of calling it right there in the bathroom, an image of the void, its blackness, its emptiness, its nothing filled her mind with promises of no more pain, no more fear, just nothing. Her vision blurred as tears welled up and spilled down her cheeks. She caressed the gun handle.

That's it. Take it, an unfamiliar voice in her head told her. She wiped her tears and looked into the mirror at the reflection of the high, narrow window over her shoulder. Through it stared the beast's black eyes . Its breath fogged the glass. It spoke. *Take the gun and end it. Come be with me and free everyone else. Why punish all these people for your failure?*

"My failure? I didn't start this. It's not my fault."

Everything that has happened today is your fault, the beast said. *You summoned me to free yourself. To escape this life of banality and want. So be free. Be nothing. It is what you are already.*

"I'm something. I'm me."

You're nothing.

The beast glared through the window. Lyn squinted shut her eyes, pressing her palms against them, but the image of the monster wouldn't go away. It remained, black eyes leering, accusing her of being everything she was: alone, inert, and afraid to free herself.

She pulled the pistol out of her waistband and spun around, aiming at the window—aiming at nothing but sunlight and trees on the other side of the glass. Her own voice echoed in her head, accusing her of not only being weak, but now, crazy. It was one thing to daydream about life being a fantasy tale; it was something else entirely to populate that life with monsters creeping in the woods, staring back from the mirror. She took her sketchbook out of her messenger bag and held it like a counter-weight against the gun in her other hand. The scale naturally tipped in favor of the gun.

She sat down solidly on the closed lid of the toilet and wept softly, holding the cool barrel of the gun flat against her forehead. The blast outside shook the window above the toilet and she screamed. And then she screamed some more.

She screamed until she was hoarse.

And then she breathed.

Still alive. I'm still alive. She thought of the monster at the window. *I'm alive and you can't have me.*

Abandoning her uniform in a pink and stained red pile on the floor, she got up, grabbed her bag, and walked out to see who was left.

She made her way along the narrow hallway hesitantly, and peeked around the corner. Despite the sound of the blast, nothing had changed. It was still a disaster—quiet and dark, except for the few spears of light shining through the holes Joanie had shot in the blinds. She stood surveying the scene, breathing. *Whatever it was that blew up, it happened in the back.* The thought unnerved her. The employees' room was their last refuge—except, everything she knew of defensible positions was just what she'd seen in the movies or read in a book about elves and wizards. Joanie knew of them from experience and training. Lyn bet she also knew how to penetrate them. "Penetrate" sounded like the right verb in her head.

She stepped around the corner and slipped behind the lunch counter, thinking she could drop down for cover if anything happened. On her way to the swinging doors, Lyn stopped in front of Carol's girlfriend's body. *Carol said she left her purse under her table. Which one was it? Table three?* Lyn walked cautiously into the dining room, boots crunching in the broken glass, and squatted down to look under the table where she remembered seating the women. There was only one purse. *Must be hers.* She grabbed it and dumped the mess of unorganized junk on the floor. Batting away everything that didn't matter to her—lipstick, wallet, a paperback book by someone named *Christa Faust* with a naked woman holding a gun on the cover—she found what she was looking for: a set of keys and a cell phone. She stuffed the keys in her messenger bag and checked the phone for a signal. Nothing. But the text message icon was green. Maybe her signal came and went like Beau's. She stashed the phone and looked for the other woman's bag in the chairs. *I bet you're the kind of woman who carries a wallet in her back pocket.* Lyn returned to the lunch counter.

Carol had gently laid out her girlfriend—*What was her name? Sylvia!*—with her hands folded on her chest next to the gaping exit wound just above her heart. Lyn bent down, plunging her hands into the dead woman's front pockets. Today was a day of firsts. She'd never seen a dead person before—not even at a funeral—and now here she was violating one by rifling through her pockets. *I'm sorry, but I bet you'd be doing the same in my position.* Lyn pulled a small cell phone out of the woman's pocket. *Voila!* It had a slide out keyboard. She popped it open and the screen came to life. Another green envelope.

And a single bar.

Lyn immediately sent a text message to her mother again. *Lyn here. New phone. Did u get other text? R cops on their way??* She hit *send* and watched the little animated envelope grow wings and fly into cartoon clouds. She only had to wait for a second before getting the reply. *What is going on up there? Called the sheriff's office. They said they'd 'check it out.'*

"God damn it! What the fuck does 'check it out' mean, Mom?" She composed herself quickly, realizing that she probably only had this one chance and no time for temper tantrums. She stood up and took a picture of Sylvia's corpse with the camera in the telephone, making sure to get the woman's wound in frame. The flash made the blood covering her chest and mouth stand out starkly against her pale skin and blond hair. Lyn hit *reply* and added *All Contacts* including Facebook to the list of recipients. She typed: *We need the police at Your Mountain Home Kitchen in Mercy Lake Idaho RIGHT FUCKING NOW!!!* Unlike last time, Lyn didn't hesitate to hit the SEND icon. She imagined that she probably sent a bunch of people more than a few nightmares, enormous therapy bills, and a maybe heart attack or two, but she didn't have any choice. People needed to know. And she needed to get word out before she lost signal on this phone, too.

"Sylvia, you just helped us more than anyone else in this place, including me." She gently smoothed the hair from the dead woman's forehead. "You probably saved Carol, too. I bet that would have meant something to you." She leaned down and kissed the woman's sticky red cheek.

She stood up, and made for the kitchen. Out of the corner of her eye, she thought she caught a glimpse of a large silhouette in the late day sun, standing near the entrance. A pain in her chest shot into the left side of her neck as one of the bodies bracing the front door open spasmed. *They're dead. They've got to be dead. I saw that man's head get...*

The corpse jerked again like the body of an antelope being torn at by a hungry lion. And then it vanished out the door. Frozen in place, Lyn waited for the beast to come back for the second body. She rubbed at her eyes with her fists. *It's not real it's not real it's not real.* Pulling her hands away, she looked at the doorway. It was still propped open. Neither of the bodies had moved since Joanie executed them. "You're not real, fucker."

An anguished howl echoed off the mountain.

Bryce was certain that it was the sound of the shot killing him when he heard the shed latch clatter shut behind him. Leonard gave him an excited shove and together they slid around the shed without being ventilated. On the other side, the men paused to exchange a quick glance. Leonard smiled and Bryce couldn't help but chuckle. The situation was taking a toll on more than their bodies. *Give it a little more time and we'll be laughing like hyenas and scratching at the bugs crawling under our skins. If Joanie doesn't kill us, we'll be too crazy to appreciate making it.* "All right. We've got cover now. I'm going in through the rear exit to see what happened. You can follow me or hang around in the lot."

"If it's all the same, I think we've got a better chance if we stick together," Leonard said.

"My thought exactly. Let's go." Bryce pulled his gun from its holster and pushed off of the wall. He jogged around to the back lot, skidding to a stop when he saw Beau lying facedown on the ground. "Jesus!" He ran up and flipped him over. Blood had pooled in the gravel and coated half his face. The top of his head was lacerated, but he was breathing. His heart was beating.

"What the fuck happened to Beau?" Leonard asked.

"I don't know. Help me get him over there." Together, the men dragged the manager toward the wall and lay him against it. "Stay here and try to wake him up. I'm going inside."

Leonard saluted with two fingers like a boy scout. On any other day Bryce would have wondered if he was being mocked. Today, it seemed sincere.

He padded back to the door and tried to open it. Locked. Standing to the side, like before, he banged on the door with the butt of his gun. No answer. He did it again. "Is that you, Deputy Douglas?" Hunter asked.

"Yeah, is everything all right in there?"

"Um, no. Is everything okay out there?" The kid pushed open the door and Bryce slipped through it quickly, his gun held up by his face, scanning the room for a threat.

"What happened in here? What was that sound?"

"Nothing happened in here. It came from outside when Luis ran away."

"Luis left? Where did he go?"

Hunter pointed out the door. "He said he was headed down the rock slide thing."

"The scree slope?" Bryce ran outside toward the edge of the lot. Looking down, it took him a long few seconds to realize he could see what was left of Luis. All over. A breeze pushed the stench of burned flesh and Luis' blown-open bowels up into his face. He fought the urge to vomit. *She's mined the woods around the restaurant. There are fucking land mines out there!* As promised, his mind threatened to snap. *Pull it together. You might not have seen worse, but it can't get any worse than it is. This is as bad as things get,* he lied to himself.

He turned around and headed over to Leonard. "He waking up?"

"No. No yet."

"Let's get him inside."

Lyn pushed through the doors holding Sylvia's telephone up over her head triumphantly. "I got through! I sent for help." She smiled, not knowing she wore the dead woman's blood on her freshly cleaned mouth, looking more deranged than before.

"Whose phone is that?" Daniel asked.

"It's..." Lyn looked over at Carol lying on her side next to Neil who was stroking her red hair. The woman lifted her face from the doctor's good leg and looked. "I went through your purse, Carol. Sorry."

"That's not mine. It's Syl's," she whispered.

"It saved us. I got messages out to my mom and everybody. They'll call the police and then they'll come and get us out of here." Carol held her hand out for the phone. Lyn regretted not deleting the picture from the gallery and sent messages folders. "I sent for the police," she whispered. The phone buzzed in her hand. She looked at it and saw that ten new messages had appeared in the in box in the last two minutes. Sending the picture had definitely gotten a response.

"Please, can I have it back?" Carol said. She crawled around from beside Neil into the middle of the room. Lyn met her half way and handed the cellular to her.

"I'm so sorry," she said. Carol took the phone and began pushing buttons. Her mouth dropped open; her face grew pale.

"What did you do?" Neil said.

"I sent for help."

Bryce banged on the door again from outside and Lyn silently thanked him for breaking the spell. Hunter ran over to let him in. Leonard followed behind carrying Beau like a sleeping child.

"Leonard!" Lyn shouted.

"Take it easy Lyn," Bryce shouted. "It's okay. He was hiding... laying low in the propane shed. It's all okay."

Although nothing was actually okay, she was relieved to see Leonard. He made her lunch and sometimes dinner at the diner. He walked her to her car in the winter when the sun went down early. He was always ready with a knowing smile when Beau made her feel her worst. He was the closest thing she had to a friend in *Your Mountain Home Kitchen*. He was back and he cradled Beau like he was there to help. The big man set the little man down gently on the floor next to Neil.

"Could you take a look at him?" Bryce asked before returning his attention to Lyn. "And, can I have a word with *you*?" He grabbed her elbow and led her down the hall before she could question what about. Lyn resisted as they got close to the swinging doors. "What is going on?" he hissed. "I hear shooting and then find out Luis ran off and blew himself up on the side of the mountain."

"Blew himself up?"

"I asked you to try to make a call, but everyone in there looks scared shitless of you. And to be honest, looking at you scares the shit out of me too! I need to know I wasn't wrong when I chose to trust you."

Lyn's head swam with the memories of the afternoon. When she'd first come to work, she was just some skinny girl who wanted to move to the big city and draw for a living. Now she was a hallucinating, crazed, gun-wielding woman who took pictures of corpses. She seized up for a moment, stiffening, and then relaxing onto Bryce's shoulder. "You can trust me," she said softly.

"I want to believe you."

She looked into his face and tried her best to give him a not-crazy stare. She guessed that she looked slightly less insane than she had a minute ago, because he didn't argue when she said, "Believe me. I'm fine."

"Okay then." Bryce looked down the hall into the mirror in the corner. Everyone in the back was watching them. "We need to come up with a plan to get out of here. No waiting. Right now."

"But I got through. Sylvia's phone works and I texted everyone. They're coming."

"Not soon enough." He stared into her face and his expression changed from that of a scared person to a cop's. *He's reading me. He doesn't trust me.*

"Joanie's wired this place to blow. There's C4 or something like it in a box wedged beneath the propane tank outside. When she gets tired of waiting to shoot us, she's going to push a button and blow this place apart." Lyn opened her mouth to protest, but Bryce interrupted her. "I'm not kidding. You may have called in the cavalry, but we've got to get out of here or else they'll have nothing to save but our teeth for dental identification. Are you receiving this?"

"What do we tell them?" She nodded toward the others.

"The truth. Once we have a plan, they get the truth." He let go of Lyn's arm and she stepped back hugging herself and rubbing where his thumb had dug into her bicep.

"So, how do we escape?"

"I was hoping you'd come up with something." Lyn felt a crushing terror that must have shown in her face. Bryce pulled her to him with his good arm. "It's okay. I'll come up with something."

They walked out to where Neil was weakly tending to Beau with Hunter and Leonard's help. It wasn't an encouraging sight. Though Neil's bleeding had stopped for the most part, it looked like it might be because he was nearly out of blood more than it was coagulating under his bandages. He looked like he couldn't carry on much longer, yet somehow, he found it in himself to care for Beau.

"How is he?" Bryce asked.

"He's alert and responsive, but he's dizzy and can't recall what happened before getting hit in the head with the door. He's most likely got a concussion, but I can't determine if he has a skull fracture or internal bleeding while I'm sitting here. We've got to get him to a hospital."

"I think I have an idea," Bryce said.

10 October 2009 — 0910 hrs — Frankfurt, Germany

Errol felt Joanie's hand twitch. He didn't send for the nurse or even get up from his seat. Despite the coma, she twitched from time to time. She'd slept for almost a month and he didn't expect her to wake up any time soon. So when she croaked his name, he almost fell out of his wheelchair.

12 October 2009 — 1154 hrs

"Are you headed back?" Joanie asked. Errol shook his head and patted his hip.

"This got me a purple heart and a ticket home. Doctors say I'll never dance again." Joanie didn't ask if he'd ever danced before and the unspoken joke died quietly. "I've been putting off catching the ride home until you woke up, but I think I've overstayed my welcome. The U.S. Government doesn't like feeding airmen who can't work or fight."

"What about the guys who did this to me? Did they get medals too?"

Errol wasn't sure what to say. In the two days since Joanie had been awake she'd seemed like a completely different person. It was understandable, but he wondered if the old Joanie would ever come out of that coma. "They're all dead, hon. Every last man. Got lit up by insurgents who thought your can was a weapons store. The way they were guarding it; I guess that's what it looked like. They took 'em all out and then when they found you inside, they locked the doors and bugged out. Probably figured you were already dead."

"Who rescued me then?"

"A few *hajjis* scavenging for leftovers. Luckiest thing that could've happened, actually. They'd pulled you out of the literal middle of nowhere."

"Lucky me." Joanie rolled over onto her side and wept for the revenge she'd never have.

21 December 2011 — 1650 hrs — Washington D.C.

Joanie fiddled with the folded up copy of the *Stars and Stripes* newspaper that recounted her ordeal while The DeepWater Corporation's lawyer reread the settlement agreement. She'd carried the paper with her for the last twenty-eight months as a sort of talisman during the litigation process. Now, it was almost over. The paper was worn and torn in places, but it still held its power over her. She intended to burn it as soon as the check cleared.

The lawyer made slight grunts and hums of assent as he went through the meaningless process of reviewing a document that he'd badgered them into revising and revising again for the last five weeks. "Fine," he said, sliding it across the oak conference desk. "If Miss Myers will sign it, we can get on with this."

"Myer. Sergeant Myer."

"My apologies." The piece of shit in the three thousand dollar suit licked his lips while Joanie did her best to eye-fuck him to death. He wasn't dying, but she felt like she was. Just looking at him made her want to crawl into a deep black pit and pull dirt in on top of herself.

She looked at the lawyer she'd hired to represent her in the civil suit against the military contractor company. Since her torturers had all been killed in an insurgent ambush, she had to name their estates in her lawsuit. As soon as the papers were filed she started receiving the angry phone calls, death threats, and once, a dummy grenade thrown through her apartment window. She was impressed with the ferocity demonstrated by orphans and widows fighting for the memory of rapist mercenaries. At the deposition, Joanie's lawyer presented the DeepWater attorney cell phone text message transcripts from two of the men describing the shipping can as "Uday's Room." *Is that a reference to the 'rape room' found at Saddam Hussein's presidential estate?* he asked. *I'm sure I don't know,* was the reply. *Is it a reference to this?* He pushed an eight by ten photograph taken of the inside of the can across the table. He'd placed yellow sticky notes with arrows pointing to the places where Joanie's blood had pooled and permanently stained the wooden floor. Twenty-four hours later they received their first settlement offer. Six months after that, they finally received one large enough to accept. Large enough for her to retire. And disappear.

All it would cost her was silence.

Despite everything else they took, she had plenty of that left.

From the conference room window inside the Washington D.C. office building, she looked at the view of the Capitol building rising over a line of bare cherry trees across the Potomac. There was no snow. Just grey. Just cold. She wanted to find a place with her own view, but not of a city river or a grand monument to bad decision making or foreign policy. Joanie craved a mountain view. Something with a lush evergreen forest that never ever, during any part of the year, resembled a desert. "Nice view," she said.

"Well, it's not the G.W. Parkway," the DeepWater attorney replied, referring to her lawyer's conference room overlooking the highway. She imagined the back of the old man's wrinkled head blowing out and coating the glass wall behind him like a bloody zit popped on a bathroom mirror. It wasn't the first time she'd imagined executing a civilian. Something had woken up inside of her after her coma—something summoned in the darkness of the shipping container, and it had a vicious imagination. She didn't find herself working too hard to banish it either. The visions reminded her of what it took to survive. They told her what she needed to be prepared to do to protect what was hers.

"Merry Christmas," the lawyer said as he handed over the check.

It was the closest she ever got to an apology.

3 April 2012, 1111 hrs — Jasper's Fork, Idaho

Another meeting with lawyers; Joanie hoped that this one would be her last. She signed the papers finalizing the cash sale of the property on Idaho State Highway 1A. Her closing attorney wrote a series of checks and passed them across the table. The seller smiled. Everyone shook hands and walked away from the table in the Boundary County Recording Office happy to be done. Joanie's first duty station had been at Mountain Home AFB in southern Idaho. She liked the isolation of the sparsely populated state, but nothing in that area suited her. It was too spare and dry. So she went north, and found the place up in the panhandle. It had cost more than she wanted to pay, especially after a bidding war with another buyer, but eventually she won (her attorney closed the deal by telling the seller she was a combat veteran paying cash, and could close in three weeks) and the house in the middle of a lush, green nowhere was hers.

She walked into the bright spring sunlight, nearly running into a giant of a man who was standing outside having a cigarette. "Excuse me," she said. "So sorry."

"No problem, darlin'. You Joan Mayor?"

"Joanie Myer," she replied, elongating the aye sound in her last name. "Do I know you?"

"Nope. But we're about to be neighbors." He spat a brown line of viscous tobacco saliva on the ground between boots that elevated him to something like six foot four or five. "Name's Adam Bischoff. You bought the house I wanted. Paid a lot more than it's worth in my opinion—not that you asked for my opinion."

She took a step back. "You're right. I didn't ask."

"Tell you what. Right now, I'll offer you what you paid, plus another ten percent to turn right around and sell it to me. Easy peasy, Japanesey."

"No thanks. I'm planning on living in my mountain home, not flipping it."

"Mountain home. I like that. I have people from down there."

"That's nice," she said, turning to leave.

"Maybe you'll get to meet them when we have the grand opening." She stopped, his comment about being neighbors finally sinking in.

"What do you mean?"

"Well, darlin', see, you outbid me on the house which I meant to turn into a rustic little bed and breakfast with all that frilly shit inside—something the wife wants to play with. But I still got the lot across the highway. Got it for a song in fact. Without the adjacent plot, mind you. Bet you didn't know that was even for sale, didja? Well, I was going to make that part a scenic overlook for my B and B guests and passers through, you know. A place to stop on the way, put some quarters in one of them coin-operated viewin' scopes and have a look at the valley. S'pose I could still do that, but a pull-over gawk spot all by itself won't make me money. Not like a cozy little roadside hotel. 'Cept now, I think I'll build me a restaurant. A little diner, like. I can call it... 'Your Mountain Home Kitchen.'" He jabbed air quotes with thick fingers. "Tell you what," he said, reaching into his pocket. "I'll even give you two hundred dollars for the name." He smiled, exposing brown-stained teeth that somehow seemed to go perfectly with his Marlboro Man big-as-a-billboard appearance. Tobacco saliva danced at the edge of his lip and he spit again. "Or, you can take my offer for closing price plus ten percent. If you don't think I'm serious, you just march your ass back in that public records office and look up Bischoff Enterprises. That's the name of the holding company my other restaurant properties are registered under. I'll wait while you do."

She stared hard at the man, trying to judge whether he was really telling her that he intended to build a restaurant an hour's drive from the nearest town, just because she'd outbid him on a house he never intended to live in. The smile and wandering eyes told her all she needed to know: he was completely serious. For a second, she thought about going inside and telling her lawyer to draft up a new Purchase and Sale Agreement. Then she thought about everything she'd gone through to get the money for her home. The beatings and rapes, the humiliation of reliving it all during a deposition surrounded by men in suits who'd never once feared for their lives, the nondisclosure and non-disparagement agreements that meant she couldn't tell her story and hold DeepWater publicly accountable.

I've outlived everyone who ever tried to take me down. I can outlast you, too.

"Thanks, but no thanks." She called his bluff. "If you serve liquor, then I won't have to get a room in town if I want to get drunk."

She got to live almost a full year in her house in peace before they broke ground.

PART FIVE: LEAVING HOME

14 July 2013 — 1730 hrs

No one spoke after Bryce finished explaining his thoughts regarding escape. Lyn felt the pit in her stomach grow larger and heavier. She thought his plan was unimaginative and dangerous; they'd already tried something like it, and Neil was bleeding to death because of the attempt. But, she couldn't think of a better idea. Bryce still hadn't mentioned the explosives in the propane shed to the people she was beginning to prematurely think of as "the survivors."

Beau sat against the door to the office holding a compress to the gash in his aching head. Since waking up, he'd asked three times, *Why are we sitting in the back of the restaurant?* Yet he seemed to be following along on some level. "There's no way I'm doing it," he offered, after they detailed their plan.

"No one's asking you to do anything," Bryce said. "I don't think you're up to it, anyway, but I can't get close without *someone's* help."

"No, I said." Beau pointed with a thumb at Neil, still resting against the wall with his son. "When he asked me to do the same thing, I knew he was trying to kill me, but at least I didn't think he *wanted* me dead. You'd think you two geniuses could come up with something that doesn't involve someone getting blown away."

Hunter leaned forward, and said, "No one's asking you to do a thing, you dick." He looked up at the policeman. "He can't be trusted to do what you want anyway. Beau's a coward. All he had to do before was stand up for a second so my dad wouldn't get shot and instead he hid behind the counter like a… like a…" Hunter struggled with the words he wanted to say, but couldn't utter in front of his father.

"I stayed behind cover. It was the smart thing to do. I didn't see you jumping out to help your old man." While his memory seemed to be

125

improving, his attitude remained bleak.

Lyn put a hand on Hunter's shoulder to calm him. "You're right, sweetie, but it's all academic anyway. Sure, Beau can't be trusted, but he can't stand up on his own either without falling down. He's out." Beau tried to stare her down, but Lyn held his gaze, attempting to burn his eyes out. He dropped his head into his hands, acting as if the pounding in his skull was why he looked away and not that The New Lyn frightened him more than Joanie did. "I *do* want you dead, by the way. If I could tie you to the front of that dumpster back there and wheel you out like a bull's-eye I'd fuckin' do it. You and Adam are the reason we're trapped in here. You're the reason all those other people out front are dead." Lyn hardened her gaze and Beau shrunk back. "I'm starting to think you should go out front with Bryce, if for no other reason than that I don't want you anywhere near me."

Daniel stepped forward and put himself in between Lyn and Beau. "Give him a break, Lyn. None of us wants to get shot." She locked eyes with the boy, forcing him into his girlfriend's arms. She remembered him from her senior year in high school. He was a freshman then, and cute, but too young for her. Plus, he was into sports and while he'd seemed like a nice guy at first, she'd been sure he'd turn out like all of the other guys who played football: not her type. Looking at Raylynne, she figured right. The girl, on the other hand, was a stranger, but she could see from the thick makeup and tall hair, they likely had little in common. "I d-don't see why any of us should go anywhere," he said. "You said you sent texts to people telling them to call the cops. We just have to wait for them to get here and we'll be okay."

Lyn glanced at Bryce, asking him silently for permission to tell. He shook his head and rubbed his eyes with his thumb and forefinger. "That's not an option," she said.

"Why not?" Daniel asked.

"Look, we need to stay calm if we want to stay alive," Bryce said.

"Spit it out! What the hell are you holding back?" Beau's face was so red it was almost purple.

Leonard stepped forward. "He's not telling you that Joanie put a bomb in the propane shed. She's got this place rigged to blow."

"Bullshit, Chief! Nobody can get into that shed without—"

"Don't call me 'Chief,'" Leonard whispered. He took a step forward. Beau's face lost its color and he drew up his knees as if he might be able to push through the cinderblock wall at his back.

Bryce put a hand on Leonard's arm. "He's telling the truth. We both saw the black box shoved under the fuel tank in there."

"How do you know it's a bomb?" Beau asked. He tried to mask the quake in his voice. "Is there an alarm clock taped to it?"

"Close enough. It's wired to a radio with an antenna and a green light and looks big enough to have a shit load of C4, or whatever inside," Leonard added.

"How do you know it's C4?"

"Explosives of some kind, wired to something that looks like a receiver," Bryce said. "Whatever's inside the box, I'm betting it sure as shit ain't Silly Putty. My guess is that she's feeling fine shooting for as long as she has a visible target and no opposition, but the minute help arrives, she'll play her endgame and push the big red button. Nobody here is getting out alive as long as we follow *Joanie's* lead."

"You've got to be kidding me!" Beau lashed backward with an elbow, hitting the wall. He squinted and seemed to swoon a little. His jaw flexed as he loudly ground his teeth without a toothpick to take the pressure.

"Feel better now?" Bryce asked.

"Fuck no, I'm not 'feeling better!' One of us is supposed to follow you on a suicide mission out the front while the rest of these losers climb down the mountain—which we've already seen is wired with explosives, too. And then when reinforcements get here, Myers drops the big one and well…"

"You need to take it easy, Beau," Neil said. "You need to calm down."

"Fuck you!"

"I suppose you can think of something better," Leonard said.

"Yeah. *You* go wait in the parking lot, Chief. I'll use the dyke's phone and call my buddy in the Air National Guard and they can napalm that cunt's place!"

Leonard's face darkened with malice again.

"That hit on the head has really pulled back the curtain, didn't it?" Lyn said. "What are you trying to prove, Beau? That you're as big an asshole as Joanie?"

"I don't think I could strip *you* of that title."

"I've had it with this grade school shit," Bryce interrupted. "Lyn, you go stand over there by Neil and Hunter. Beau, if you want to live through this, you are going to have to trust me. And stop antagonizing everyone. You're going to climb down the rock slide with Lyn and the others. Daniel is going to run interference for me and draw her attention."

"Why me?" Daniel asked.

"I've seen you play football," Bryce said. "You're fast. You've got the best chance of getting behind cover once you catch her eye."

"I can't outrun bullets or bombs, man!"

"All I need is her looking one way while I go the other. If I can get across the highway, well, maybe nothing will blow up."

Daniel folded his arms to hide his hands tremble. "You'll have to knock me out and drag me out there. I'm not doing it. I'm staying with Raylynne."

"I'll do it." Carol stood up, wiping her face although her tears had dried long ago.

"Are you sure?" Lyn asked.

She nodded. "I've got nothing left to lose."

"How come nobody asked me if I was sure?" Beau said.

"If what they said about you and the guy who owns this place is true, then you're the reason Syl is dead!" Carol shouted. "I'd help Lyn tie you to that god damned dumpster!"

"But she sent that picture of—"

Carol held up her phone for Beau to see. "And since she did I've gotten a dozen messages from people all around the country who've been calling the police to come help us. I have friends in *Europe* who've been on the phone to the cops here. What have you done to get us out of this?"

"What have I done? You've been catatonic since I dragged your ass behind the lunch counter!"

Lyn lurched at Beau, raising a bandaged fist for another shot at his nose, hoping to break it this time. "*I* helped her behind the counter, you lying bastard!" Bryce caught her arm and held her back. "Since this whole thing started you've only been interested in saving your own ass," she shouted. "You deserve to be the one who looks like a boxer, not me!"

"None of this is helping us get out of here," Bryce said, dragging Lyn toward the hallway.

"I'm not helping him out of here. Fuck him!" Bryce gripped her face with his good hand and gave it a shake. She thrust her knee into his balls and shoved him away. The cop stumbled back coughing, cupping his groin, looking like he might be sick. "And fuck you too if you think you're going to knock me around like he did."

"I just wanted your attention," he gasped.

"My name is Lynnea Lowry, god damn it. And I'm nobody's punching bag. Hear that everyone? If you want something from me, you say my name and ask me, pretty fucking please."

"Please, Lyn. Help us," Neil said. "Help *all of us,*"

"Yeah, Lyn. Please," Leonard added.

Carol said it with her eyes. For the first time since Lyn started working at the restaurant, people looked at her with something approaching actual respect. She wasn't sure what to think. She felt changed. Maybe they saw it, too. Maybe they just wanted to be on the side of the crazy woman with the gun—the *other* crazy woman with the gun. Shoving past Bryce, she shot another poison look at Beau and said, "I'll help. Everyone. Even you." A day ago she'd never have kicked a cop in the balls, and if she had, she'd be crying and begging for his forgiveness. *He should feel lucky I didn't crush his nuts a second time. And I* like *Bryce.*

While the others bickered over who was leading the group down the mountain and who was following, Carol slipped into the dining room. She pushed through the swinging doors and crept onto the killing floor. She found her purse where Lyn had left it with all of her things strewn around. Silently collecting them, she placed each of her possessions carefully back into the bag. None were things she needed anymore, but she felt like she should gather them up all the same.

She stood up straight and looked out the front door. From where she stood, she could only see part of the parking lot and the woods beyond. And the blood. And the bodies. She turned away and went behind the lunch counter where Sylvia waited.

Kneeling on the greasy rubber mat, she set her bag next to her lover's hand. "Hang on to this for me." The joke came unbidden. She was a joker—had been her entire life—why stop now? *Because there's nothing left to smile about, that's why.* Looking up, she found a damp rag dangling off of the counter. She pulled it down and tried to clean some of the blood from Sylvia's face. Most of it was drying and caked on. Only enough came away to stain the rag so that successive dabs just smeared the blood around. She stopped trying.

"I'm so sorry, Syl. I would take you out of here with me if I could." She considered what they had planned. She and Bryce were going to race across opposite sides of the parking lot—Carol high and making a commotion, Bryce low and quiet, sneaking across the highway to the shooter's house. She was supposed to dash behind a car and take cover. *And then do what? Bryce plans to run across the street while I... what? Fumble in my pockets for my keys? Maybe I could check my lipstick in the side mirror and straighten my hair. Fuck it. It's as good a plan as any other I've heard.*

She caressed the dead woman's face and tenderly stroked her side as she moved her hand to Sylvia's left wrist. Carol slipped the plain titanium band off of her wife's hand. Syl had complained that it was loose since she had lost weight. Even though titanium bands like the ones they'd bought couldn't be resized, she refused to replace her ring with one that fit better. Keeping the original meant too much to her. That was the one she'd promised until death do them part with. Carol turned it over in her fingers and read the inscription inside: *7/14/03 Family of Choice.*

"I think I know what I'm doing. At least I know what I want. I guess we'll see if I have the guts to go through with it. I volunteered anyway, because if I didn't that girl who took your picture would have volunteered. I don't know her, but it seems like the sort of thing she'd do and ... I don't know. I've had enough of sitting back and watching her take all the risks. I can do this one thing. And I know you can't see me, but I'm going to pretend you can. And I'm going to try to help. I'm going to try to do the thing you would have done. I love you, Syl." She leaned down and kissed her wife on the forehead, not able to bear the thought of Sylvia's lips not kissing her back. She stood up and, staring at her feet, walked toward the swinging doors, trying not to look at the other dead bodies littering the dining room. She bumped squarely into

Bryce standing beside the lunch counter in Joanie's blind spot. Watching.

"What are you doing?" he asked. He was looking at her the way so many strangers had during their trip out to visit Syl's family in Moscow, Idaho. He scowled at her with equal parts judgment and pity.

"I'm just saying goodbye." She rubbed at the side of her neck, trying to find something to do with her hands other than claw at his disapproving look and rip it away.

"Look, I know it is hard for you to lose your... friend."

"My *wife*."

Bryce stared hard at Carol for a moment before continuing. "If you're going to be my backup, I need your head in the game."

"My head is where it is. I'm what you've got, for whatever that's worth."

"We're getting ready to head out back and give it a shot. But first, will you pray for forgiveness for your sins with me?"

"You think I'm a sinner?"

"We all are. We're born in it," he said.

She shook off his unwelcome touch and shoved past him. "You can ask for forgiveness if you want to, but I've got nothing to atone for."

As she pushed through the doors and into the back, she heard him whisper, "I do."

Standing at the edge of the back lot, Lyn and her team stared at the rocks below. She tested one of the boulders with the toe of her shoe, timidly at first and then pushing harder. It didn't move. She was pretty sure that wouldn't be the case all the way down. Hunter and Leonard stood on either side of Neil, holding him up. His right pant leg was soaked with blood. Standing there in the setting sun, the exit wound looked much worse than it had indoors. Again, what would have turned Lyn's stomach a day ago, or even earlier this morning, didn't now. *How quickly a person can change.* She checked his tourniquet and asked, "Are you sure you can make it?"

"I don't have many other options, do I?"

"Nope."

"Then I can make it." He was pale and out of breath, but upright.

Beau leaned against Daniel and Raylynne as they huddled in the middle of the lot whispering to each other. Lyn felt some of her old uncertainty and self-consciousness peek through as she feared they were talking about her. Then she put it behind her. *Who cares what they're saying? When we get to the bottom of this rock slide I'm never going to see or talk to Beau or either of them again.* She resolved at that moment to take a friend up on her offer to come visit Oregon. *Adam and Beau can't blackball me in restaurants as far as Portland. I can start fresh. I just have to make it down the mountain.*

Bryce and Carol were having trouble moving the dumpster to the edge of the building where it could give them an additional bit of protection and a little extra attention to the north side of the diner while he sneaked past the propane shed on the south. But it fought them. It wasn't made to roll in the gravel, and no one ever moved it. Usually, Beau and a couple of guys he picked up at the Home Depot parking lot would empty the garbage from the bin into the back of his pickup before taking it to the dump. Even if they got it into the position they wanted, Joanie's shots seemed to punch through everything. Lyn didn't know if they could penetrate a dumpster half-full of garbage, but she'd seen them go through plenty of other things inside the restaurant: skulls and tempered storm windows and pretty much anything else in their way. Maybe she was using armor piercing bullets that'd Swiss-cheese Carol's cover, too.

"Do you really think that's going to help?" Lyn called out.

"It has to," Bryce said. "I can't think of anything else."

"I have an idea," Leonard said. He leaned over and whispered in Lyn's ear, pointing at Beau. Although she didn't smile when he finished, she thought that under any other circumstance she could have kissed him.

"Beau," Lyn said. "Beau," she repeated, louder when he appeared to ignore her. She walked up behind him and tapped him on the shoulder instead of cuffing him in the back of the skull with her gun. "Give me the keys to the basement?"

"What for?"

"I want to grab one of those Fourth of July rockets you have down there."

"We fired them all," he said. "On the Fourth."

"Leonard says you held a bunch back."

"That's stupid. Why would I save any?"

"Because nights you work late, you pop one or two off before heading home. Because you're a petty, small shit of a man who *enjoys* torturing the woman across the street. You think if you drive her out of that house, Adam Bischoff will finally agree to give you what you want—whatever that is—partnership in the business, a stiff dick up your ass, I don't care. Now give me your keys or I'll take them from you."

"Try it, if you think you can." His challenge was almost comical given that he looked like he was doing his best not to vomit and pass out from the exertion of standing under his own power.

"Jesus Christ, Beau," Neil called out. "When you're standing in a hole, stop digging."

He shouted, "Stay out of it, nigger." A silence fell over the lot while everyone stared at Neil, waiting to see what a man who'd lost too much blood could do when pushed hard enough.

"No one has called me that to my face since college," Neil said. "Absence doesn't make the heart grow fonder, you know. Go ahead and shoot him, Lyn. Please."

Abandoning the dumpster, Bryce ran back to intervene. Holding up his hands he said, "Come on, Lyn. Leave him alone. He's a shit heel and he'll get what he deserves eventually."

"Yeah? How's that? Is a karmic lightning bolt going to come out of the sky and fry him? Is the Almighty Lord going to send him to Hell for being a coward *and* a racist? I'm not banking on my imaginary friends to do what needs to be done." Her imaginary friend was no help at all. Not lurking at the edge of the woods the way he was. Staring.

"I'm not a racist. He just got under my skin with that crack—"

"No? He was trying to tell you to shut up before you said something stupid. And then you went and said something dumber than anyone could have imagined." Lyn said. "Because you're a racist moron. I'm saying it plainly because you're too stupid to get it any other way." She saw him balling up his fists, his knuckles turning white. *Come on. Hit me again. I've got something for you.* "Got something to say, dummy? Having trouble using your words?"

Bryce shoved Lyn back a step. "Lyn, shut up. Beau, give me the damn keys." He held out his hand. "I won't ask again." Beau handed them over without backing down from the staring contest with Lyn. "Here, take them," Bryce said, tossing them in the gravel at Lyn's feet. He held his breath while her hand hovered over the butt of her gun. Beau blinked and looked down. She picked up the key ring.

Far off in the distance, Bryce thought he could hear a siren. If he was right about Joanie, they were running out of time.

Lyn started flipping through the keys until she found the one for the cellar door.

"What good is a firework going to do anyway?" Bryce asked.

"Joanie can shoot through the dumpster," she said. "Your idea is going to get the two of you killed before you even get started. But we're still going to create a diversion for you. I hope you can run as fast as you think you can."

Lyn emerged from the cellar with a small mortar tube cradled in her arms like a very heavy infant. "We're going to fire this at one of the cars," she explained. "Even if it doesn't blow up a gas tank like in the movies, it should still be a helluva show set off at ground level. Enough of one for you to get to your patrol car. And then what?"

"And then I try to stop this before she shoots a state trooper, or a paramedic, or blows the side of the mountain off," Bryce said.

"And the rest of us?" Daniel asked.

"You're leading the group down the mountain," Lyn said.

"Me?"

"Yeah. You. All you have to do is go first and don't break your neck slipping on..." *Luis' guts.* "...the rocks, or set off any mines," she said, adding the details that had made her most fearful of the original escape plan. She looked at Beau's cowboy boots and figured he probably wouldn't be able to get farther than two or three boulders down before he twisted his ankle and tumbled the rest of the way into a trip wire or a pressure mine or whatever Joanie had rigged up. She shocked herself again by thinking, *And if he does that, he just clears another safe, albeit messy path for the group. It's a win-win.*

Bryce looked at his backup team and asked, "So what's the signal?"

"Signal?" Lyn and Carol both asked.

"Yeah. The signal for me to start running."

Lyn held up the rocket. "This isn't enough?"

"I suppose it is," he said. "Which way are you going to shoot it?"

"The couple with the dog had a nice car. I think I'll torch that one," Lyn lied. She intended to wreck Beau's pickup.

Bryce looked at her with narrowed eyes and then held out his good hand. She took it and gave a firm shake like her grandfather had taught her. He winced and she wondered whether he could run at all with that kind of pain in his shoulder, let alone deal with Joanie on the other side. Still, he was the only one with the training to put an end to this. He was their only chance.

1755 hrs

Lyn and Carol crept along the side of the building, staying as flat against the wall as they could. Bryce's blood trail leading out from under Andy's pickup was dried and brown. "Where are you going to fire it from?" Carol whispered.

"Right here, I guess. I haven't thought that far ahead." Lyn looked at her targets. She had a clear shot at Beau's truck if she stepped into plain view. She considered aiming for Joanie's front porch instead, but she wasn't sure how the rocket would fly or when it would explode. It wasn't like one of those rocket propelled doohickeys in the movies. The thing was made to go on the ground and point straight up. Holding it in her hands, she figured it might make it across the street if she had time to figure it out. She had a better chance of hitting something close.

"Do you even know how to light it?"

"Duh! I just light the fuse right here..." Lyn turned the tube over looking for a fuse. Instead, she found a pair of copper wires tucked inside the bottom of the cylinder. "Fuck! There's a battery or something, I guess." She turned to run back into the cellar to figure out how to launch the thing.

Carol grabbed her arm. "No time."

"We're got plenty of time," Lyn said. "Bryce won't go until we give the signal. I can go back and—"

"Once he's in front of the shed, he said she can see him. We can't wait." Carol stood up.

"What the hell are you doing?" Lyn hissed.

Carol started jogging toward the lot. "Creating a diversion. He'd better get moving. She's pretty fast with that gun."

"Come back," Lyn screamed. "He doesn't have a signal!"

Leonard did most of the work helping Neil over the rocks. Though strong, Hunter was too small to be of any real help with him on the other side. As soon as he had to scramble off of a boulder that shifted under their weight, the two big men were left holding each other. While he labored near the top, Beau and Daniel were already halfway down the rockslide. Beau had shrugged off Daniel's aid and was moving down the rocks on his butt, leaving them all behind. *Just like Lyn said he would.* Behind him, Daniel had decided it was better to help Raylynne than go it alone; he was more or less carrying her down the mountain—lifting her off a rock, putting her down, apologizing, and then climbing down another and pulling her off the next one. When Leonard heard Lyn's distant voice call out to Carol, he had to resist the urge to go back up. He wasn't a coward, but when the shooting started he'd taken his grandmother's advice to never run toward disaster. He'd found a place to hide and hunkered down to wait until the threat either found him or left on its own. *I guess that does make me a coward.*

It was something he wanted to make up for.

Carol ran into the parking lot, fighting the instinct to hide behind one of the cars parked there. She'd thought she was out of tears, but at the last minute, found a few more, and her vision blurred with grief and fear, making the run even harder. She'd gone along with Bryce's plan, knowing it was suicidal, and then the girl tried to save her. Again.

She ran to the tailgate of the giant pickup truck and paused, waiting to see if she could hear Bryce running along the opposite side of the lot. She couldn't.

Taking a deep breath and hoping it wouldn't hurt too much, she stood up as straight as she could and calmly walked into the parking lot with her hands up. The silence seemed to stretch out like a thick blanket that covered the world, muting everything. No birds, no traffic, only her heartbeat and the sound of feet in the gravel.

"Hey! Over here, you bitch!"

And then she felt the hit.

Every step down the mountain was hell on Neil's wounded leg, but he continued. He didn't want to prolong the experience by slowing down. As if he could. *Any slower, and I'll be standing still.* Nevertheless, something was telling him not to move forward. To hunker down and wait. He pushed on until Leonard came to a stop, looking worried.

"What is it?"

"I don't know," Leonard said. "Just a feeling." The big man held up a hand and called out to the others farther down the slope. "Daniel! Raylynne! Wait!" The two high school kids turned back. Leonard gestured for them to stop. Beau didn't look. He called out again. "Beau! Stop!" The little man kept crab-walking down the mountain, reaching the point where Luis' remains began.

"What's the matter?" Neil asked.

"Bryce thinks Joanie's got a switch for the bomb in the shed."

"Yeah. That's why we're down here," Hunter said.

"What if it's connected to whatever she planted down there too?"

"Jesus," Neil whispered. "Beau! Stop!"

"Over here, you bitch!"

Out of the corner of his eye, Bryce caught a glimpse of Carol's bright red hair. He glanced over to see her standing beside Beau's Silverado pickup truck waving her arms. *Jesus! What's she doing? Where's the damn fireworks?*

Taking it as a signal, he ducked forward, keeping his head low as he sprinted away from the side of the building, trying to stay as close to the tree line along the far edge of the lot as he could. He assumed something must have gone wrong with the rocket. It was the only explanation why Carol would be standing in the lot trying to get shot.

Unless that was her plan all along.

He lost a step as he looked up and saw the place from which Joanie had to be launching her assault. Unlike the windows on the main floor and the upper story, which were obscured with white sheer curtains, the windows at under the deck patio were completely blacked out. *It's a shooter's blind. She's perfectly concealed. She can see out, but we can't see in.* He imagined her set up behind the black curtain, watching them from under the cover of the deck. He realized when he'd first pulled into her driveway, the stairs had to have blocked her view of him. *If I'd stayed put instead of running to help those kids, I could have made it in and stopped the whole thing then.* That had never been an option for him, though. He had as much choice then as he had now to stop, to find a place to hide, to leave everyone else behind and sneak away alone.

He thought he might be able to pick out the faintest silhouette of his lover behind the blind. He staggered a couple of steps, staring into the black hole at the base of the house before pushing forward again, knowing he couldn't afford to stop. Knowing that Joanie would be taking her shot at Carol any second. And after that...

The Lord is my strength and my shield; my heart trusts in him, and he helps me.

Carol dropped out of sight as he ran toward a pickup truck that would give him another second of cover before he had to race across the open highway. He saw a flash of light from behind the black screen. His breath disappeared in a sensation like being punched hard in the chest. He tried to draw air in but there was none around him and he was being pulled into the darkness.

He'd seen her and she had looked back, and made her choice.

He lost the feeling of his body, and his legs went limp. He fell dead in the gravel. No more regrets, and no account left to settle with either his wife or his lover.

The shot echoed through the valley like a fresh peal of thunder.

He never heard it.

Carol hit the ground, grit digging into her arms and face. She struggled to take a breath and couldn't; dust choked her and got in her eyes. She pushed up, trying to stand again—wanting to give Bryce the longest diversion possible, but it wasn't in her. Her body was too heavy.

I'm so sorry, Syl. I love you so much! She had wanted to grow old with the woman she'd married at Cambridge City Hall. Barring that, she was going to die young with her.

The weight of her body lightened and the pain receded. A tinge of hope tinctured the moment as she realized that she didn't feel gun shot. *I'm just out of breath. This isn't so bad.* She got a small breath of air that smelled and tasted like the mountains—not the parking lot—actual pine and birch. The chilly late afternoon air cooled her tongue like fresh stream water. And then the pain came flooding back as a pair of hands clamped around her wrists and started to drag her through behind a truck.

She heard a rifle report. It sounded like a door slamming in Hell.

Hunter asked what they should do. He and Leonard looked to Neil for answers. Neil had none. Medical school had never prepared him for this. Leading a crisis team in the E.R. was nothing like leading a group of terrified people down a booby-trapped mountain rockslide. He'd only wanted to spend a week in the rental cabin with his son before returning the boy to his mom in Seattle—to spend a few days with a boy whose time with him was already too short and infrequent.

"We'll wait and see if Bryce's plan works, I guess."

"How will we know if it did?" Hunter asked.

Neil pulled his son closer. "I don't know. My guess is we'll find out sooner if it doesn't."

"How so?"

"The mountain will tell us," Leonard said.

Beau slipped on the tacky, gore-covered rocks, but persisted. His head swam and his stomach threatened to rebel. He couldn't remember most of the details of the last few hours, but he had the big picture well-conceived: *Get off the fucking mountain before the crazy bitch across the highway makes it your grave.* Whatever they were discussing behind him didn't matter. *I'm done with their little committees. I'm getting out of here.* Lyn's accusation that he enjoyed torturing Joanie was still stinging. He knew the fireworks would push her, but he didn't enjoy it. Every summer they drove his own father into seclusion in the basement, shivering and trying not to think about the jungle. The old man spent the last week of June and every Fourth of July drinking himself into oblivion in front of the plasma TV watching the quietest thing he could find: golf. Every pop, bang, and rocket-shriek buried him deeper in some claustrophobic Vietnamese tunnel, battling rats and Viet Cong with bottle after bottle of whiskey. Beau figured that Joanie would take the same self-destructive route. *So much for expectations.*

Beau planted a foot on a rock that felt steady and eased himself down a little more. It shifted beneath him as he put more weight on it. He slipped and fell, landing on his back on the apex of the boulder. Despite the pain and the dizziness, he forced himself to get up. He was far beyond the point where Luis had met his end. Yards past the black scorch and the red spatter. *Almost home free.*

Except he wasn't.

The shifting stone had brought him face to face with a slender black wire extending across his path. He followed it with his eyes and found the surprise waiting for him at the end. It dawned on him why the others had been shouting.

Weighing his options—back up with the others or over the wire—he chose the latter. *You can do this. Get on the other side of it and into the woods. Don't let the bitch pen you in.*

Lyn had never tackled anyone before. Carol's body broke most of her fall, but it still hurt. By instinct, she'd stuck out her already lacerated palms to catch her weight, and spare Carol some of the force of their landing. The small jagged stones jabbed into the bandages, and her arms immediately buckled from the pain. Carol's elbow rammed into her guts and knocked the breath out of her. She rolled to her left, kicking with her heels and scrambling beside the truck. Carol lay still in the dirt, choking and puffing up dust. Lyn leaned down, grabbed her wrists with her aching hands, and pulled the woman into the space between the truck and a station wagon with Massachusetts plates. Carol rolled over and doubled up, sputtering and choking. Mud caked her face in streaks where she'd been crying.

"Are you okay?" Lyn gasped. "Can you talk?"

"What did you do?" The question crushed Lyn a little. It was the second time someone had asked her that and both times the answer was that she'd hurt a woman who had never done anything to her.

"I couldn't let you do it. There are too many people dead already." Lyn leaned against the Subaru and wondered if it was Carol and Sylvia's. Carol rolled over and grabbed hold of Lyn's hand. She said nothing while she lay there sobbing. Lyn wasn't sure if she'd done the right thing or not.

Either way, this is it. I can't drag her any further. If Bryce doesn't get over there before Joanie sets off the bomb, we're all dead. She peeked around the car, looking for him along the path he'd have to take to get across the highway. He wasn't there. She hoped that meant he was safely on the other side. A little further up, she saw his boots sticking out from behind a car. He lay still.

She lost hope.

"Oh God. He didn't make it," she said. Carol didn't respond. She lay in the gravel fighting to catch her breath. "What do we do now?"

"Die," Carol said.

Lyn tried to get Carol to look at her, but the woman rolled over and curled up on her side. "I'm so sorry."

"For what?"

"For Sylvia. For taking that picture. For everything. Everything is fucked and I don't know what to do anymore."

The sirens in the distance were growing louder. Carol said, "I understand why you did it. I can hear why you did it."

"I'm still sorry."

"I'm not going to forgive you." The words made Lyn's stomach knot a little. She wasn't fishing for absolution—at least she didn't think she had been. She decided that she didn't need to press the issue. In their present circumstances, neither one of them was going to feel better by having a long conversation about it.

"We need to get out of here," Lyn said.

"If we get up, she'll shoot us."

"If Bryce was right, when those emergency trucks get here that bomb goes off and it won't matter if she wants to shoot us. Personally, I'd really rather not burn to death."

"So go ahead and go. I'm staying here."

Lyn pleaded with Carol. "Come with me."

"Why?"

"Because... Because Sylvia would have wanted you to live."

"You didn't know her."

"Am I wrong? You said she would have taken a picture like that to save us. If she would have done that, I bet she would have wanted you to run for your life, too. But if you can honestly tell me that Sylvia would have wanted you to kill yourself instead, I'll leave you here."

Carol turned to face Lyn. "What's your plan?"

"Joanie's."

Carol's eyes went wide and she shook her head.

"For real. We make a run for it and try to get behind her place. Hopefully, she hasn't rigged her own house to go up, too, and it'll be far enough away from an explosion and..."

"And what?"

"You wait. Hide in the trees behind her house. And then I go in. I need to try to talk her down."

"What if she doesn't want to be talked down? What if she shoots you?"

Lyn patted the gun in her belt, but didn't feel any of the confidence that gesture was meant to inspire. She tried to swallow but couldn't for a long, panicked moment. The thought of facing down a trained killer made her want to shut down. She forced herself onto her haunches and held out a hand to Carol. "I'm going into the woods and around."

"What do we do for a distraction?" Lyn spotted the fireworks mortar she'd dropped. It had rolled underneath Beau's truck. She teased it forward with the tips of her fingers until she could get a good grip. She slinked backward with the prize in her hand and sat up. Tearing a long strip off of her blouse, she unscrewed the gas cap off the truck and stuffed the cloth in as far as she could. She dug out the lighter she'd intended to use on the mortar and lit the end of the cloth, tossing the mortar in the bed of the truck. "Think we can get some fireworks?"

"You're out of your mind!"

"You coming?"

Carol nodded. "I'm right behind you."

"Run *beside* me or I'm not going." She looked at the scrap of poly-cotton blend burning quickly. "Better make up your mind quick."

Carol got up on her haunches and grabbed Lyn's hand. Together, the women launched themselves out from cover and into the woods bordering the lot. Something in the corner of her eye moved, and Lyn slowed a pace to look over her shoulder at it. The thing—*Kreewatan*—stood in the brush to the side of the restaurant, its lupine face leering at her.

A blast of hot wind from the gas tank explosion buffeted her and a piece of hot shrapnel embedded in the tree next to her. The fireworks mortar went next with a screech and a deafening pop. The beast let loose a howl that would have rattled the windows of the café if they hadn't been blown out already, and Lyn, for the first time since the siege began, felt true despair— like she'd seen how her life was about to end. Carol yanked her arm.

"Come on!"

1800 hrs

Joanie scanned the lot looking for more people. At this point, there was only one person left that she truly wanted to make certain died by her hand. But Beau didn't come running out behind either Bryce or Lyn. Of course he wouldn't.

Hearing the faint sirens in the distance, she gave up on prolonging the standoff any further. For all she knew, Beau had been the one who triggered the grenade she heard go off earlier, and he was already dead and gone. She'd have to learn to be satisfied with his conceptual demise. Now, it was time to wait for the cavalry to arrive. And when they did, she'd show the whole world what it cost to have her home.

She looked one final time through the scope at the spot where she'd last seen Lyn and the other woman. She didn't want the girl to suffer. She spotted them dashing away from the parking lot into the woods. *Run, Lyn. Run for it. I'll let you go.*

Taking aim on the woman sprinting beside her, Joanie said, "Another person is about to die because of you, Adam. Was it worth it?"

Then, the fireworks started and her mind shut down.

They dashed across the highway not looking to see if a passing semi on the road would do Joanie's job for her. *It'd be an easier way out,* Lyn thought, imagining the bulldog grill of a Mack truck crushing her body and flinging it far up the asphalt. Despite their carelessness, the women made it across. They kept running through the woods to the rear of Joanie's house.

They paused at the back porch, gasping for air. Lyn wanted to keep running all the way around the house, around to Bryce's cruiser on the other side and simply drive away. She could intercept the other emergency vehicles and tell them not to come up. Warn them about Joanie's trap. Then, she thought of Neil and Hunter and Leonard and all the others on the side of the mountain. *I can't leave these people here to die.*

"I'm going in," Lyn said, unconvincingly. "You should wait over there in the trees. Get far away from everything." She didn't say that she'd be back soon, because she didn't believe it.

Carol shook her head. "I'm coming with you. You don't—"

"It's what Syl would've done." Carol grabbed her hand and squeezed. Lyn didn't argue. She squeezed back and took a deep breath to marshal her courage.

Hand in hand they crept up the steps as quietly as they could manage, Lyn tried the back door. It was unlocked. *I guess Joanie didn't expect anyone to make it past the parking lot.* She let go of Carol, unzipped her boots, slipped them off, and set them next to the door before letting herself in. Carol followed suit, kicking off her shoes as well. They padded through the house in their stocking feet.

Lyn had no idea where they should go; she'd never been inside Joanie's place before. Then, she heard the screaming.

"Incoming! We're taking indirect!"

It came from downstairs. Next to the stairway leading to the second floor, she found a panel push-door. Carol gasped and squeezed Lyn's arm painfully. Glancing over her shoulder she saw the white dog lying beside the table in the breakfast nook. A pool of semi-congealed blood spread like a cozy maroon blanket underneath it. *Joanie loved that dog.* Everything seemed so much bleaker in that moment. Joanie wasn't just erasing the diner. She was erasing everything in the world around it too, even the things she loved most. Lyn suddenly lost hope that Joanie hadn't also rigged her own house to explode. Looking at the dog, it seemed like a certainty. *This is the end of the world as Joanie intends it.*

Her legs stiffened and refused to move. *It's just a couple of steps, Lynnea. Think small. The world is a little tiny thing and the end of this whole ordeal is only a couple of steps away. You just have to keep moving forward.* Except, her grandfather's advice had never been intended to lead her into danger. It was supposed to lead her home. At that moment, she wanted the distance between the top of the stairs and what awaited them below to be too great to overcome. A cosmic gulf that would take lifetimes to cross. She realized, that's exactly what it was. The space between upstairs and down, was very likely all that remained of a lifetime.

Turning away from the dog, toward the screams, she popped the door latch and pulled it open, revealing a narrow set of uncarpeted stairs heading down. She pulled the gun from her belt and thanked her good fortune that it hadn't fallen out as she sprinted through the woods.

With Carol hugging her arm tightly, they started down the stairs. Halfway down, the screaming tapered off. Joanie was getting herself under control. They could hear her panting and sobbing, but she'd stopped screaming. Lyn couldn't tell if that was a good or a bad thing. She continued down the stairs, thankful that none of them creaked under their weight.

She hadn't counted on the chirping "nightingale floor" in the hallway.

"Shit! Do you think she did it? Did she blow up the restaurant?" Hunter asked.

Leonard, perched uncomfortably on a wobbly boulder, considered the question. The explosion was followed by a familiar squeal and a loud bang. "No," he said. "That's Lyn's Fourth of July rocket."

"Plus something else. That wasn't just a firework," Neil said. They watched as some of the boulders shook and smaller rocks started to tumble down the slope. Leonard and Neil looked at each other and shared a thought. "I'm pretty sure when the diner goes, this scree slope is going to turn into a rockslide. We need to go back up. Head into the woods up top and hope for the best." Neil looked at Leonard and Hunter for confirmation. They nodded.

Leonard stuck his pinkies in the corners of his mouth and whistled at the others, farther down the mountain. Daniel and Raylynne stopped and looked up at him. He jerked his thumb over his shoulder to signal that they were headed back and waved for them to follow. Raylynne pulled at her boyfriend's jersey, encouraging him to ignore them and keep going down. He half-shrugged and turned to follow.

"Let's go," Hunter said. "Either they're right or we are. Someone's got to make it home alive. Right?" Leonard nodded and hoped his face conveyed agreement with the sentiment rather than what he really thought.

The three of them started back up. It was slower going and harder than their descent. Gravity had done half the work lowering Neil down the rocks.

Now it fought them. As they neared the top of the slope, Leonard felt his stomach clench and his heart began to race faster. He stopped dead with Neil and stuck out a hand to hold back Hunter. From above it was invisible, but approaching from below it was right there for anyone to see: another black plastic box stuck under a boulder. A red light on the side of it glowed in the shadow with cyclopean menace. This one was smaller than the toolbox in the shed, but he felt certain it was big enough to do the job.

"What's that?" Hunter asked.

"It's a bomb," Leonard said. "She wants to start an avalanche."

"Will it do that?"

"She seems to think it's worth a try," Neil said. "I don't think we should wait to find out. Let's go around."

Hunter looked down the slope at the others. "What about them?"

"They're almost to the bottom. They'll be all right," Leonard said, trying to convince himself more than the boy.

Lyn held her breath and stared at the door in front of her. The muffled sounds coming from the other side told her that passing through this door was a final act. Merely opening it meant confronting Joanie. Probably getting shot and dying. Turning away meant they still had a chance of escape. She and Carol could run into the woods and let the police stop Joanie. *Except they can't. She's going to blow everything up unless we... I stop her.*

She remembered Neil, crouching under his table. While she knelt in broken glass, he'd asked Hunter what it was they did when they were able. "We help people," She whispered.

She couldn't walk away and do nothing. She had to try.

She slid Carol's hands off her arm and reached for the knob, hoping it would be locked, wishing for a reason to creep out of the house and leave in Bryce's car. *If it's locked, what do I do? I can't break it down.* The latch clicked and the door swung silently open on its well-oiled hinges.

At the far end of the room, Joanie sat on the edge of a wooden platform pointing a pistol at them. Lyn regretted not searching Bryce's cruiser first. *He probably had a bulletproof vest in there.* Lyn kept her own gun in hand, hanging at her side.

Joanie didn't say a word as the women stepped into the room and let the door swing shut behind them. She sat, staring, brows knitted in confusion. Lyn thought she could see a hint of the kindness she'd shown on her infrequent visits to the restaurant. Unfortunately, that look was buried beneath more than a hint of the madness she expected to see in the face of a woman who'd just gone on a killing spree.

The room was Spartan: unpainted drywall and dusty concrete floors. Along one wall was a workbench covered in the remains of whatever Joanie had used to set her remote control explosives: wires, clippers, black electrician's tape, and a couple of spare batteries. Resting on the workbench nearest the shooter's platform was something that resembled a piece of armor. Gray and sectioned into rectangular bars, it looked like a combination of a corset and a therapeutic brace and... something else. Lyn realized when she saw the wire emerging from the top what it really was.

She made a fucking suicide vest like those bombers in the "martyr" videos wear. An image of a woman dressed in green holding up a rifle and a religious book flashed in her mind. *Was she going to walk into the restaurant and set it off, or was it for when the police get here?* Lyn didn't want to know the answer. Either way, Joanie hadn't put it on yet, and she hoped the dangling wire meant it was inactive. If it were to go off, she wouldn't have time to regret not running away with Carol in Bryce's patrol car.

Behind them, she heard panicked grunting and a sound like a struggle. Lyn didn't dare turn around, but when Carol whispered, "JesusfuckingChrist," in her ear she knew it wasn't good.

"Can we talk first, or are you going to shoot me?" Lyn asked.

Joanie tilted her head to the side, considering her options. "I don't know what we have to talk about. But if it makes you feel better, I never wanted to hurt you." Lyn looked at the bandages on her hands. Despite the ibuprofen from the restaurant med kit, they hurt like hell. Everything hurt. "What happened to you?" Joanie asked. Lyn almost laughed at the absurdity of the question.

"I had to crawl through glass to get the blinds down."

Joanie smiled. "Yeah, the blinds. That was a ballsy move. I hadn't anticipated you doing that. It slowed me down." Her eyes narrowed. "Who's she?" she asked, gesturing at Carol with the .45.

"She's my backup." If Lyn was being truthful she'd have said, *She's here so she doesn't kill herself.*

"Cute."

"Real backup's coming, Joanie. Can you hear them?" Lyn paused so the sound of the sirens could bleed into the room. "It's over. You can stop now."

"Nothing's over. We're still alive." She raised her other hand. Clutched in it was a black stick topped with a red button she held down with her thumb. A little light on the side blinked green.

"What's that?"

"It's a dead man's switch."

Lyn's stomach did a somersault. She didn't know the term, but she figured out the principle quickly enough from the fact that Joanie had already pressed the button and nothing had happened. *If the psycho lets go of the button, the bomb in the restaurant goes off—and maybe the one on the workbench, too.* She realized that her hastily devised plan was as futile as Bryce's had been. *If she shoots me, I drop the gun and she goes ahead and does whatever else she has planned. I could shoot her, but then she drops the switch and she still gets what she wants.*

"Why are you doing this? What can you possibly stand to gain from... all this shit?"

"I'm doing it for revenge."

"Revenge?" Lyn remembered her epiphany behind the restaurant and knew the real reason why. But that still wasn't worth murdering innocent people. She didn't know how else to put that to the woman in front of her. It all seemed so absurd. "For what? For building a restaurant? For wrecking your view?"

Joanie stared at her hard. "Do you think this is about a fucking view, Lyn? Sure, they took that and made it something obscene. I could live with that, though. Nothing's perfect. But it's the whole psy-ops campaign, Lynnea. They destroyed what was left of my peace. I can't sleep. They blast my house with music like I'm some Central American dictator hunkered down in a bunker. That sonuvabitch Beau McCann fires off a rocket every fucking night."

"I know." Lyn wished that she'd pulled more than one rocket from the cellar. *A full-on show might have bought us more time.*

"They've taken everything away from me but this house, and now they got that, too. Tomorrow, the judge'll hand it over, and I'll lose the last thing in the world that was mine. To him!" She jabbed the gun at the presence behind Lyn. The women flinched but Lyn didn't turn around. "Go ahead. Look. I won't shoot.

Lyn turned and saw Adam Bischoff tied to an uncomfortable looking high back dining chair. He stared at them with terrified, bovine eyes. A hiss of breath escaped through the gag in his mouth. But he didn't whimper. Next to him, on a small table, sat his phone.

Lyn's stomach cramped and a smothering guilt crashed into her like a wave breaking against rocks. She remembered the text she'd sent. She'd fantasized about him rolling up in that Beemer of his and get out looking like he'd just won the lottery. And then... She pushed back against the image. *That's not who I am. I didn't send the text because that's not who I am!* But she *had* sent it.

Lyn turned away. "What the fuck, Joanie!"

"I'm sorry about getting you mixed up in this. I really am. But sometimes people get hurt when they're not supposed to. They're just doing their jobs and trying to make it home at the end of the day, and then everything goes to shit. And you don't ever get back what you've lost. You get pushed out of line and you can't start over. You're just out, on your own!" Joanie was punctuating her sentences with the switch. Every movement of her arm made Lyn cringe.

"People aren't *getting* hurt, Joanie. You're hurting them." In reply, Joanie fired the pistol at the wall behind Lyn's head. She and Carol both screamed. The sound of it concussed Lyn's eardrums and deafened her. She flinched and tucked down, squinting her eyes. When she opened them again, Joanie hadn't moved even a little bit.

Joanie's voice sounded miles away when she spoke, like someone on a radio turned down too low. "I lost everything before I even moved here. I did everything right. I served my country. I went to war, Lyn. And what did I get for that? A medical discharge after being gang-raped."

The revelation hit Lyn like a sucker punch.

"They destroyed my insides. The doctors had to cut it all out. But I did the right thing. I went to court to get justice and I won. I used that money to buy this place. A place where I could be alone and heal. And what? That whoreson behind you decides that he can have whatever he wants so he builds that fucking dump you work in to drive me out. And when I don't roll over, they start bombarding my house with the fucking fireworks. So, I go back to court, like a good citizen, and you know what? He buys his way out of it!" Joanie jerked forward, shaking the dead man's switch at her prisoner. "So here we are. Beau McCann waiting to die in his diner and Adam Bischoff sitting here with a front row seat thinking about his wife and—"

"What about *my* wife?" Carol said. The sound of her voice lingered in the air like the echo of a long musical note. Joanie shook her head trying to clear the ghost of the question from her ears.

Nothing I can say will keep her from letting go of that button, Lyn thought. She tried anyway. "If you went to this trouble, why not pick up Beau this afternoon and have it out with the two of them personally? Why ruin everything for everyone else? What did *I* do? What did Carol do? There are other people out there who haven't lost everything yet."

Joanie's hard expression cracked and she smiled—not with relief, but incredulity. She laughed. "They will."

"Why do you get to be the one to decide that?"

"Because I'm the one with the *gun*." She shifted her aim toward Adam. She glared at the man shivering in his chair, trembling a little herself. Closing her eyes, she leaned her head back and listened as the sirens got louder and were joined by the sounds of screeching tires in front of the house. "They're here," she said.

Lyn looked out the window over Joanie's shoulder to see the ambulance pulling in front of the restaurant. Beyond that... the thing from the bathroom window... from her sketchbook... from the woods... it waited next to the propane shed, black eyes promising that this wasn't the end. Its blood red tongue snaked out and licked at frightfully long teeth. It was hungry.

Staring out the window at the thing, Lyn raised her gun. "Please don't do this, Joanie. Please!"

Joanie let go of the button.

In the second between the beep and the boom, Lyn squeezed the trigger.

Leonard, Hunter, and Neil, moving like a three-legged race, ran through the trees until the blast knocked them off their feet. The heat of the explosion washed over them. Leonard smelled his hair singeing, but he was alive. Pieces of the restaurant began to rain down through the trees and he felt Hunter jerk on his sleeve, trying to get him to stand up, shouting something he couldn't hear. Leonard pulled himself up and more pieces of debris crashed to the ground around them. He looked through the burning trees at what remained of *Your Mountain Home Kitchen*. The blazing ruin was half collapsed. On the highway, an ambulance lay on its side, and someone—he couldn't tell if he was a cop or a paramedic or a firefighter—ran in circles, on fire, screaming while his friends tried to put him out. Finally, Hunter's voice penetrated the dull hum of his deadened eardrums.

"Leonard! Please! Help my dad!"

He saw Hunter kneeling over his father. A small triangle of blackened steel jutted out of the man's back. Neil wasn't saying anything.

"Help him," the boy cried.

Leonard picked himself up and began to run through the debris, toward the highway to get help.

The boulders above them shuddered and began to tumble down as the explosions shook the mountainside. Daniel clutched tightly at Raylynne as they slid toward the tree line with the avalanche. "Keep running," he cried, but his words were swallowed by the thunder of the stones pushing them down, crushing them.

The howl of the explosion echoed off the mountains into the forest below and the ground trembled under his boots. Beau ran as fast as he could through the woods, barely careful enough not to clothesline himself on a low branch or break his ankle tripping over a raised root. The rumble reminded him of the childhood tale of the giant who'd slept so long he'd been covered by grass and trees and become another mountain. He laughed as he ran. He laughed as he soaked his Wranglers with piss imagining a fiery, tree-covered behemoth towering above him, looking for a tender morsel with which to break the centuries-long fast.

"There's a restaurant back there," he shouted at the burning giant. "It's *Your Mountain Home Kitchen!*"

Beau despaired, but he didn't stop running until his legs gave out and he collapsed in a heap at the edge of a large, clear pond. He knelt in the mud on the bank of the water and sobbed into his hands. The surface of the water was calm, as if the world hadn't just been ripped open.

He cried and he waited for his sins to catch up to him. By sundown, when no one came, he got up and walked back to the diner, letting the light of the fire guide him.

Lyn, red faced from the heat of the blast through the open window, picked herself up off the floor and looked at Joanie lying in a pool of spreading blood. The woman choked and sputtered as the wound in her throat frustrated her attempts to get air into her lungs.

Sobbing, Lyn stumbled over to Adam Bischoff's overturned chair, stooped down, and unbuckled the strap around his face. He spit out the dog ball. "Jesus H. Christ! She did it! Untie me. Let me the fuck out of here!" When Lyn paused at the straps holding down his wrists he bucked hard against the chair. "What are you waiting for? Untie me. Let me go right now!" She took a step back and looked at him. "What? What are you waiting for?" he asked.

"I want an apology," Lyn said.

"An apology! She's the one that—"

"I want to hear you say that you're sorry."

Adam Bischoff pulled against the ties holding him to the chair until his hands turned purple. He shouted for help. "In here! Come on! I'm in here!" Lyn held a finger up to her lips.

"Tell Carol you're sorry her wife died."

Adam's eyes widened with rage. He twisted up his face and shouted, "You're as crazy as she was." He began to kick and buck. Lyn took a step back, getting the impression that whatever impact Joanie had intended to have on Bischoff's perception of himself and others, it hadn't taken. He was the same. Everything had changed for her and everyone else inside *Your Mountain Home Kitchen*. For everyone outside of it, life continued on as it always had. She imagined that there would be news reports and dissections of Joanie's life and her motivations. They would talk about out-of-control violence in the culture, without ever addressing the real problems that made people do cruel and horrible things. But when the news cycle wound down and a new source of fascination emerged to take the place of the old, nothing would have changed. Life would lurch on until the next senseless tragedy. And the one after that.

The smell of smoke drifted in through the window. Burning pine and rubber and scorched earth assaulted her senses. She blinked against the stinging breeze, trying to focus. The sounds of sirens outside, the screaming and shouting brought her back to the present.

You can put out fires, but that doesn't get rid of fire. You just survive if you can.

"I'm in here!" Bischoff shouted again. "I need—"

Lyn saw Carol out of the corner of her eye only a second before the woman pulled the trigger on Joanie's .45. Twin red blossoms bloomed in Adam's torso.

"Jesus! What are you doing?" Lyn shouted.

"She said it was all his fault," Carol said. "He started everything."

Lyn stepped away and gently took the gun from Carol's hand. She pulled the woman close and held her. Carol let her hands hang at her sides as she stared down at what she'd done.

Adam Bischoff groaned, unable to get his breath. Drowning alongside Joanie.

He hadn't *started* tearing down Joanie's life. But he'd been intent on finishing the job, and brought in the wrecking crew. Lyn was part of that plan.

She'd helped him get his wish. Joanie lost everything and Lyn had a hand in it.

There is no end to horrible things.

So what do you do? How do you live in a world like this? She thought about Joanie's attempt at a fresh start. She said she'd done everything right and nothing paid off. It was all for nothing. *I can't accept that. It has to be worth trying. It has to be worth holding together.*

She wiped Carol's prints off of the pistol grip and the trigger with her torn shirt and returned the weapon to the dying woman's hand.

"What are you doing?" Carol said.

"I'm trying to hold it together. Trying to give us both a second chance."

She held Carol's hand tightly as they walked upstairs and out the front door, leaving Adam Bischoff and Joanie Myer staring at each other for the rest of their lives.

Together, they walked out of the only thing Joanie couldn't bear to see destroyed.

10 October 2013 — 1801 hrs

The newsreader on the television with her perfect hair and sun-wrinkled cleavage recounted the lead story of the last several months. "With a hot summer drought and uncleared forest debris providing ample fuel ready to burn, the wildfire that consumed Gunsight Peak was the largest in Idaho's Boundary County in over seventy years. It took firefighters from both the Bureau of Land Management and volunteers from British Columbia until the first snowfall this week to finally get the blaze under control. Although officials say the fire is now one hundred percent contained, they estimate the cost of putting out the conflagration to be close to one billion dollars. Twenty-two homes have been lost. Six people, who refused the order to evacuate, are dead. The human cost of the tragedy, which began with the Mountain Home Massacre, continues to rise." The anchorwoman's eyes sparkled as she said, "Mountain Home Massacre."

Cherie winced at the words. Real people's pain reduced to a B-movie tag line. And that was just the local station. She didn't have the heart to follow national coverage who'd picked up the phrase and run with it. When she refused to open the door for them, the big networks lingered outside her house until her dad made a plea for privacy. Surprisingly, they'd respected that, and left. Although the phone, on occasion, would ring. There was a rumor that Mark Wahlberg was going to star in the movie. People talked about him buying a place in Sun Valley.

She turned off the television in the kitchen and called her kids down for supper. She still set a place for her husband, even though Bryce wasn't ever coming home. Cherie pushed her food around her plate and watched her kids eating their supper in silence, and wondered what they'd think of her if they knew what she'd done. If they knew she'd made him go up there to put things right with his mistress. That *she'd* sent him up the mountain. To them, he was the first responder—the helper—the fearless man who'd raced into the line of fire to help innocent people. She promised herself he'd always be the helper to them.

A knock at the door interrupted their meal. "You want me to get it, Mom?" Logan said. Annie glanced at the door fearfully. She'd been the one who answered when Sheriff Winter had come to give them the news. For weeks after, the sound of the bell made her burst out in tears.

Cherie dropped her napkin next to her plate and, "No. You two stay put. I'll see who it is." She got up to answer it and found Steve Pullman waiting on the other side, a white Stetson hat in his hands.

"Sorry to drop by unannounced," he said. "But no one answers the phone." He stood on the stoop waiting, not asking to be let in.

"I'm glad to see you," she said. It was the truth. "We're just sitting down to supper. Would you like to come in and have something to eat?"

"Only if it's no trouble. I don't want to impose; I just dropped by to make sure you and the kids are doing all right."

"It's no trouble at all." She stepped aside and motioned for him to come in. He smiled and walked through the door before pausing to give her a big hug and tell her how sorry he was. He glanced over his shoulder at the children sitting at the table. And the empty plate.

"Are you expecting someone else? I can go."

"No," she said, pulling him toward the empty chair. "It's for you." Bryce hadn't been gone long, and she was sure the neighbors would talk. But then, it felt like a lifetime ago and it was good to have another warm body at the table. Someone to talk to.

Kreewatan moved on.

EPILOGUE:

13 June 2018 – 1445 hrs

Lyn turned the envelope over in her hands. Mail like this—real mail in the real world—represented time lost, time ahead, time that she'd never get back or under control. Envelopes were heralds of mortality carrying news of progress toward the finish line. Births. Weddings. Funerals. Once released into the world you couldn't take them back. They traveled with purpose, alive only as long as it took for them to reach their destination and then they were ripped open, cast aside, dead—their irreversible work done.

She looked at the return address before opening it: Portland, Oregon. Slipping the slender blade into the gap at the fold, she slit the harbinger open, spilling its contents on the table like an offering to the gods of time. A white card with an embossed image of a blocky building stared up at her. Around it was printed the legend, Lincoln High School, Class of 2017. She opened the card and stared at the image of the man Hunter Tate was becoming. He was tall and handsome standing in a blue robe with his mortar tilted at a funny angle atop his prematurely graying, kinky hair. Despite his smile, Hunter's expression was imbued with a look of native sadness that didn't belong on a face so young or handsome—so like his father's. A woman stood beside him. Lyn recognized her from the contents of other envelopes that delivered moments dragging her forward with them. His mother. She stood behind Hunter's father, Neil, who was seated, as always, in his wheelchair. Despite what the piece of shrapnel lodged in his spine had done, his face projected absolute pride and a vitality that belied his dead legs. Legs he'd sacrificed to the god of fathers and sons.

All gods were gods of death, even when they gave life in exchange for blood and careers and legs. They gave life that was marked in moments marching toward an inevitable bargain—*all this I give in exchange for death. Eventually, I will touch you and take away all the moments you have left, leaving your family with one last envelope to fill.* Who can say no to the gods? Who can say no to their appetite?

Lyn slid open the drawer in the center of her desk and slipped the announcement on top of Hunter and Neil's other mail, none of which ever received a reply. She took the photo into the kitchen and stuck it to the refrigerator with a magnet shaped like a bottle of champagne. Next to it hung the picture of Leonard at his doctoral hooding. He towered over his advisor, one arm around the beaming man's shoulder, holding up his degree in his other hand. The corner of his mouth tilted upward slightly, forming the broadest smile she'd ever seen him wear. She missed his cooking.

Joanie Myer had pushed them all in different directions. Once a doctor, once a cook, once a waitress. Now, all different. Transformed by the pain a single woman sent hurtling into the world with gunpowder and fire and agony. Blood washed some of them clean, exposing new bright identities, gleaming with hope and potential. Some. Not all.

With a ragged, bitten nail, she gently traced the soft line of Carol's cheek in the picture hanging beside Leonard's. Carol had made it three seasons until the god of lovers demanded what she'd promised him in the parking lot of *Your Mountain Home Kitchen*. Printed beneath the picture, 1983-2013, and a slightly uneven line where Lyn had severed a prayer from the rest of the card with a pair of scissors. She burned the prayer in the sink, setting off the fire alarm in her kitchen and inviting a threatening call from the landlord.

The smell of smoke reminded her of once-upon-a-time, when she met a dragon.

Grabbing her backpack, she went out the back door, down the dim stairwell three flights, and out into the postage stamp yard behind her building. She paused beside her meager garden. The vacant lot behind her building allowed her flowers all the sun they needed. They grew tall and beautiful and strong. No block of brick and concrete to cast their yard into shadow. No one else in her apartment cared what she did along the fence so long as they had room to store their bikes and a couple of barbecue grills.

Some developer had put up a sign in the lot advertising the latest round of urban renewal and deluxe condominiums ready for sale. That meant more people who wanted to enjoy the bohemian atmosphere of an artist's neighborhood from the bland comfort of a cookie-cutter plain white box. It was only a matter of time before her building was sold, the tenants evicted, and it was gutted to make room for people with more money than taste. The smells of incense, paint, and turpentine would be replaced by expensive perfume and the musk of a hundred toy dogs too lazy to walk because they'd been raised in handbags. Her dream home lost to the shallow desires of others able to pay for atmosphere rather than create their own.

She dug in her pocket and pulled out her knife. Flipping open the "speed-safe" blade, she used it to cut a stem of white blossoms off a branch. Emerging from the alley beside her building, she stepped out onto the busy sidewalk and crossed the street without looking. A cabbie stood on his brakes and honked. She didn't hear. On the opposite sidewalk, she turned and walked up the block to the small diner where Suzanne worked.

Inside, some new girl at the hostess station told her she could sit anywhere. She sat at one of Suzanne's tables and smiled when the girl brought her the greasy, laminated menu and water in a cloudy plastic glass. She ordered lunch without looking at her options; Suzanne smiled and sauntered off to put in the order.

The waitress was tall and slender. "I work here, but really I'm a ballet dancer," she'd said once. Lyn had never seen her dance, but she moved like she floated an inch above the floor—like she was too light to touch the ground for more than a second. Lyn stuck the asphodels in her water glass and pulled her sketchbook out of her messenger bag. She leaned over and put the finishing pencil touches on an image of a woman about to face off against a vampire or a werewolf or whatever shit paranormal villain, a.k.a. boyfriend, inhabited the novel they'd slap her cover on. The warrior with Suzanne's face stood ready for battle in a corset and a pair of leather pants, peeking over a bare shoulder at her creator while holding a katana in one hand and a gilt cross in the other. Her days as a dancer were over; now she was a slayer of demons. Lyn penned the warrior in with ornate Deco whorls and curls topping a Mucha-inspired arch that made her think of fantasy woods populated by lithe immortals with unmarred faces and unspoiled love for all living things.

People nothing at all like her.

"Hey! That's cool. Is that me?" The waitress leaned over Lyn's shoulder. Her approach in the noisy diner had been too soft for Lyn to hear.

"Do you want it to be?"

"It looks like one of those covers for a Heather Langdon novel or something. You know the ones?"

"I do," Lyn said. "I work for Punctured Publishing. She's one of ours."

"Wow. That is so awesome!" Suzanne leaned in closer. The manager barked at her to "hustle." She ignored him, instead peering at the sketch of herself cast as an action hero—the woman who saves the day.

"If you want, when I'm done with the painting, you can have this sketch."

"For real?" Her face lit up like a little kid's. She wasn't much more than a kid. Lyn wished she could still find it in her to feel that light and excited about something as simple as a drawing. But she'd left that part of her in Joanie's basement. It was part of the price she paid to live. She thought of the pictures of Carol and Neil on her fridge and the prices they paid. She thought about Beau, "drinking himself to death," according to her mother. That's what the guy who wrote the book about their ordeal never understood. They'd all paid a price to survive. Some paid all at once and some on the installment plan. Some, like her and Hunter and Leonard had come out ahead.

Lyn would burn the world black to keep it that way.

She gave Suzanne her cell number and then ate her food quietly before tipping double the bill. After lunch, she wandered out onto the sidewalk in front of *Deluxe Uptown Diner* and looked at the tall buildings towering over her. She gazed up at the sky above them filled with hazy white clouds and imagined the invisible stars beyond. Giant gas planets and burning behemoth suns and black holes eating them all, and took comfort in how small they all really were. She loosened her grip on the knife in her pocket and stepped off the curb to head back home where, at least today, she had a perfect view of the city she loved.

HOME RESTORATION: an afterword

This re-release of *Mountain Home* is more than just an "author's preferred" or "unexpurgated" edition, but a kind of updated restoration, like remodeling a home. What you've just read is the culmination of a line-by-line revision that both brings the book forward to a point that I think better reflects my current prose style, without changing any of the original content (well, maybe one small detail—did you catch it?), while also looking backward and reinserting the original, cut ending that better reflects my intention to create a thoughtful (if violent) portrait of two women on opposite sides of a mirror from one another.

Why did I want to do that? Let me give you a little background and I'll explain.

This isn't the first book I've written (I wrote three others before this, that'll likely all remain in the trunk for very good reasons), but it is the first book I sold. Though I had interest from some traditional New York agents and editors based on my pitch for the novel, everyone I approached in legacy publishing passed on the book for one reason or another. Some of the reasons were understandable. For instance, while the book is novel length as defined for awards purposes (i.e., greater than 40,000 words), it's a short novel and therefore less viable in genre publishing, where "marketable length" for thrillers hovers in the 70,000 to 90,000 word range. For those of you who count in terms of pages instead of words, that's roughly 280 to 360 pages. As you can plainly see, this book is shorter than that.

Other reasons I didn't agree with as much—and a couple I thought were just plain wrong—but I won't go into detail about them here. Suffice it to say, there's no arguing when an agent turns you down. A no is a no, and you pull on your I'm-a-Professional pants and move on. Eventually, the editor of a small Canadian press liked it and bought it.

It being my first time at the dance, I was uncertain about the editing process and how vigorously I should or could defend the work that had gone into the novel while he was suggesting changes. Most of the editor's comments about the book were excellent, tightening the story and making it better. But there was one big edit I disagreed with: he wanted to cut the Epilogue.

We had a discussion about that, and his reasoning was that it put too nice a bow on the story, and "made a five-star book into a four-star book." My response was something to the effect of, "Well, you're the publisher; you know what you're doing, I guess. I'll take your word for it." And I let him cut the end of the story.

That publisher then hired the wonderful team at Small Dog Design to do the cover (that to my delight, remains on this edition of the book), and we released it. For the most part, the response to the original edit was wonderfully positive, with a few exceptions. One particularly motivated reader wrote me a five-page e-mail telling me everything he hated about the story, and another took me to task for getting the details about the Glock handgun *technically* correct, but not detailed enough to his liking (there's another lesson in there, called "you can't write for everyone"). But, I always felt uncomfortable about the last line of the book being "Kreewatan moved on." Yes, it's poetic, and it wraps up the thematic subtext of violence as an unstoppable constant, but it left unresolved what happened to everyone after the explosive end of the siege. In the first edition, the reader never gets to know what happens to Neil, Hunter, Leonard, Carol, and Lyn. Some of them are obviously *alive* in the aftermath, and some, well, we don't know. I *like* open endings (I like also to call them "French Endings"). But that wasn't my intent here. I didn't want to write a completely French ending for *Mountain Home* and leave the reader with too many unanswered questions. That never sat right with me. After what Lyn and the other survivors have been through, the reader deserved to know at least whether or not they got out of the woods.

Here and there, I gave a few people an errata sheet that I printed out containing the missing Epilogue. Almost universally among that audience, the opinion was that the book was better *with* the expanded ending than without. So, when my original publisher made the decision to streamline their back catalogue and release a few authors from their contracts early, I volunteered for the chopping block so that I could have the chance to publish this novel the way I intended.

As I mentioned above, I left the original story intact. I contemplated bringing it closer to the present, but while I think Lyn's story is moveable, Joanie's part of the tale is linked in my mind to a certain period in time. And for her, I think it's important that it remain there. The real world issues revolving around Joanie aren't resolved by any stretch of the imagination and are still contemporary, but she feels like a part of the immediate aftermath of the wars in Iraq and Afghanistan. I wanted her to remain close to being in war, and to the wounds she received there. And that meant leaving the book set in 2013.

I mentioned above that I did alter one other detail of the story. In the originally published version, Lyn contemplates sending a text message to Adam Bischoff to lure him up to the diner and possibly his death, but she doesn't hit *send*. She tells herself, "that's not who I am." A year or so ago, I had a conversation with a reader, and friend, who thought that it would have been more provocative if she *had* done that. That text, having been sent, does a lot of things, not the least of which is demonstrate that there's a very real possibility that Lyn could come out of this experience badly broken and pushed further down the road toward eventually becoming like Joanie. It also introduces earlier in the story the idea that Joanie has given Adam a front row seat to the horrors she's inflicting, when *she* gets the message sent to his phone. I don't like revisionism, and I argue strongly against the constant re-edits of *Star Wars* and the idea of making changes like replacing guns with walkie talkies in *E.T. the Extra-Terrestrial*. But in this case, I think my friend was right. I'd missed a chance to muddy the waters and make Lyn a little less of a perfect protagonist, because I was afraid to get her too dirty. So, now, she sends the text, firing her own shot at one of the people responsible for her pain. If you prefer the original where she doesn't hit *send* (I suppose my version of "Han shot first"), I hope you'll forgive me. I honestly think it's better this way. Though your mileage may vary.

I could write so much more about *Mountain Home* and what it means to me (and how it served as the springboard for other books like *Stranded* and

13 Views of the Suicide Woods), but I think it's best that I leave this, like the novel you just read, a little short. There's something to be said about letting the material speak for itself instead of spending too much time dissecting it and laying it open for all of its flaws to come spilling out. What I do want to say is this: if this is your first time reading this book, I hope you enjoyed your visit to Your Mountain Home Kitchen, and that you'll come back to read me again real soon. If you bought the original edition of Mountain Home, and now this one too, I want to thank you doubly. I appreciate that you spent money that could have gone toward a meal or a movie on a second version of this story instead. Moreover, I truly appreciate that you gave me a few more hours of your life to revisit these characters who mean so much to me.

Thank you for reading!

Bracken MacLeod
Cambridge, Massachusetts
17 July 2017

Bracken MacLeod has worked as a martial arts teacher, a university philosophy instructor, for a children's non-profit, and as a trial attorney. In addition to Mountain Home, he is the author of the novels, Stranded, and Come to Dust. His short fiction has appeared in several magazines and anthologies including LampLight, ThugLit, and Splatterpunk and has been collected in 13 Views of the Suicide Woods, published by ChiZine Publications. He lives outside of Boston with his wife and son, where he is at work on his next novel.

Also available from

CPSIA information can be obtained
at www.ICGtesting.com
Printed in the USA
LVOW13s1715230518
578238LV00013B/1090/P

JUN   2018